LIFE IN A SAVAGE LANDFILL

By

Michael Evanichko

LIFE IN A SAVAGE LANDFILL
By
Michael Evanichko

Internal and cover illustration
by Thomas Gaadt

This book is a work of Fiction. Names, characters, events, or locations are fictitious or used fictitiously. Any resemblance to actual persons or events, living or dead, is entirely coincidental. This book is licensed for private, individual entertainment only. The book contained herein constitutes a copyrighted work and may not be reproduced, stored in, or introduced into an information retrieval system or transmitted in any form by ANY means (electrical, mechanical, photographic, audio recording or otherwise) for any reason (excepting the uses permitted by the licensee by copyright law under terms of fair use) without the specific written permission of the author.

Edited by Denna Holm

Publishers Publication in Data
Evanichko, Michael
Life in a Savage Landfill
1. Fiction 2. Illustrated 3. Suspense 4. Humor 5. Thriller 6. Action Adventure 7. Mystery

ACKNOWLEDGEMENTS

Thank you to my friends and family for their amazing support during the book tour for my first novel, *Life in a Supermarket Basket*, including Kevin Moore, for facilitating and managing several book signings and selling more copies than I ever imagined possible. Thank you to Miranda Miller and Denna Holm for saving me years of self-editing by providing thorough and necessary editing notes. Special thanks to Krista Morelli and Sandy Zech for their consistent pom-pom shaking, and to all who have shown their support by reviewing my work on Amazon and other online outlets. All of this support and love encouraged me to continue writing *Life in a Savage Landfill*, book two in the trilogy of LIFE. I also wish to thank the following geographic coordinates which brought out the storyteller in me: Folly Beach, SC, and Hocking Hills, OH. In the words of my literary hero, Stephen King: *"The primary duty of literature is to tell us the truth about ourselves by telling us lies about people who never existed."*

Contents

Life in a
Savage
Landfill

THE GIRL

In the dream, she was buried alive. This wasn't a shallow grave with dirt layered directly on her body, nor was she in a wooden coffin protected from the earth and all its slimy inhabitants. She was pinned down by unknown objects while tiny gaps in the darkness exposed the light of day and allowed air to permeate the burial site, which didn't comfort her much. And for the first time ever in a dream, she had the sense of smell. It was putrid and nauseating, recalling her first time in an outhouse while camping with her cousin. Never mind her physical state, as the worst part about this dream was the stench.

"Help!" she whimpered, quite sure of being unheard. "Help me, please!" This one had the force of slightly more lung power. And then she decided to bypass the *being saved* part of the dream and just wake the hell up from it. In the past, if she concentrated and willed it enough, she successfully awakened from nightmares.

Happy images helped, so she tried to visualize a cute puppy jumping through a field of weeds. It wasn't appearing. She saw the field and the wildflowers but no fluffy pup. For this twelve-year-old girl, it was sometimes hard to create happy images. At age six, she'd questioned why her parents were so much older than her friends' parents. By age eight, she learned the horrible truth; she was being raised by her grandparents. The aunt and uncle she saw once a year were her mother and father. This sent her young psyche into a spiral of rejection, self-loathing, and a general hatred for the other kids in her school who hadn't been tossed aside by their birth parents. She also treated her substitute parents poorly, resenting them for not telling her the truth of her abandonment sooner. The dream and the horrible odor drew all the negative energy from her real life and created a volcano in her head—a volcano unable to erupt, for it was capped by a huge mountain boulder.

And then the puppy appeared, jumping over the tall weeds, running through the field without a care in the world. Helen smiled, knowing she would soon awaken in her cushy bed, the only aroma being scrambled eggs and sausage. She waited and waited. This was taking longer than usual. The puppy stopped running and started barking. Suddenly, the large, scaly foot of a *Tyrannosaurus rex* landed on it and smashed the poor thing into a bloody pulp. At that precise moment, Helen Redfield realized she was not dreaming.

She really was buried alive.

"Help!" she yelled with much more force and purpose. Her life now depended on getting help. She squirmed and freed her right hand, which was tucked behind her, and used it to push the heaping pile of unknown objects up a smidge. In the process, her middle finger was pierced by something metallic. She screamed and kicked simultaneously, and her right foot emerged from the burial site. A warm breeze tickled her exposed toes, and she discovered she wasn't buried all that deeply. She pushed her leg out a little more, which cleared some rubbish, causing her body to shift a little. If only her left hand was freed, she might have a chance, currently pinned down by a wooden object. She took some deep breaths, which were difficult to pull through her mouth but not impossible. Her head had a little bubble of freedom.

What was happening? How did she end up in this rank place? Her mind rewound to the last thing she remembered….

◎　　◎　　◎

The ringing bell above her head signaled the end of the last period of school, and the end of the school year. Helen couldn't be happier. This was her second attempt at sixth grade. She'd been held back because her grades sucked and because she had a terrible attitude. She also liked to kick the asses of her male co-students. Bad skin and greasy hair made her a shoo-in for bullying and poor treatment, but she fought anyone who messed with her, forcing the kids to talk amongst themselves and mostly keep their distance. She was befriended by a couple of students, though.

Chance caught up to her in the hall. "What are you doing this summer?"

"Sleeping." Helen hoped to get out of the building without hearing the fake goodbyes and brag-worthy summer plans. Vacationing in Europe and spending the summer with grandparents in Florida were plans she'd already heard the popular girls talking about. Helen didn't have to go to Florida to spend time with her grandparents.

"Who are you sleeping with?" he asked and then chuckled.

"Not you, ass face!"

Helen liked Chance. He was cute with his ripped jeans and combed-back, curly brown hair. They shared a connection; perhaps it was their ability to match levels of sarcasm and cynicism.

They continued down the chatter-heavy hall. "I'm spending my summer in the French vineyards making wine," Chance said. A friend high-fived him.

"You heard Susie too then." Helen rolled her eyes. "What an asshole!"

"I know, right? Hey, we should hang out this summer."

Helen was surprised. While friendly in the confines of the prison for learning, Chance never asked to do anything with her in the outside world. He was a friendly, cool, nonjudgmental boy. Why did he want to hang with a loser like her? She was skeptical. Was this one of those movies where the popular boy bets his friends he can score with the ugly chick and turn her into a beauty?

"I told you I'm not sleeping with you." She smiled at him, but just for a second. She couldn't allow it to linger, for that would reek of desperation. She was interested in Chance but needed to proceed with caution. And the sex jokes were lacking substance. She wasn't interested in that yet and would have no clue where to begin.

"Ha ha. Let's ride bikes or something."

"Ride bikes? Really? Who does that?" She laughed. "Oh, wait. You do. Sorry."

She'd seen him riding past her house a few times, as he had a friend on her street. What appealed to her the most about this boy was that he didn't fit into a mold. He wasn't into the latest and greatest video games or football or most other things boys his age were into. He was in the higher realm of popularity in their class of roughly six hundred, but he never seemed to allow it to go to his head. He, too, acted like an outcast when he was around Helen, as it seemed they were both trying to find their fit in the puzzle of life. They could be perfectly matched misfits if given the opportunity to figure it out.

Sadly, that opportunity might never come to fruition.

They stopped at Helen's locker, and she grabbed all the contents, which weren't much: a few books, a lightweight jacket, headphone speakers, and a chocolate bar. No pictures of Justin Bieber or One Direction.

She slammed her locker door. "Do you have to stop at your locker?"

"Nope. Ain't got nothing."

"Wow. You're a loser."

Chance hugged a couple of kids and high-fived another as they headed to the propped-open glass doors at the front of the school.

"Yeah, who's the loser now, girl? At least I have friends!" He playfully punched her arm, and she pushed him away. They left the building. "Hey, why aren't we Facebook friends?" he asked.

"You never requested. Besides, I hardly ever get on there."

"You're a snapper, aren't you?"

"Oh yeah. I love making myself look like a dog. Or a reindeer. That's so dumb."

They stopped at Chance's bus, and he faced Helen. He opened his arms and held them out. "Let's hug it out, bitch!" She rolled her eyes and walked into his arms, allowing him to hug, but not really hugging back.

"I'll Facebook you. We'll hang." He quickly jumped on the bus.

"Excuse me, young lady. Can you help me?" Helen turned to find a tiny old woman. She looked about a hundred years old. Her dark brown eyes were the only color appearing in her ashen, wrinkled face.

"Yeah?"

"I seem to have lost my glasses, and I can't see a foot in front of me."

Helen wondered why the woman hadn't been flattened by a school bus if she was that blind without glasses. "Okay. Where were you when you lost them?"

Buses started pulling away. Helen spotted her bus on the other side of the parking lot and saw it was still loading. She had another minute.

"If I knew that, I'd know where they were now, wouldn't I?" The old lady was being rude in needing someone's help. Helen wasn't bothered, though, as this actually made her laugh. This woman nearing death was still sassy.

"Good point. Where do you want to look?"

The lady quickly but cautiously walked past her and around the side of the school. Helen followed, wondering how she was moving so fast.

"I was back here," she said.

The old woman stopped in her tracks as Helen walked around her, peering at the grassy ground of the mini courtyard. She heard buses pulling away from the front of the building, but on this side, there were no buses. There were no parked cars. It was just the two of them. Old woman and Inspector Helen, or Detective Redfield, if you will. Except she wasn't that great at solving mysteries. The missing glasses weren't showing up. And this investigation had to end immediately, or she'd be walking home.

"I'm sorry, I have to go. I'm gonna miss my—"

The woman screamed and fell to the ground. Helen rushed to her, leaned over to help, and then the screen went dark. The plug was pulled on her memories.

◎   ◎   ◎

Helen's mind raced as she struggled for air. *Did the school explode and collapse on me?* They'd had bomb threats in the past. Had some little asshole made good on his threat? If that were the case, help should arrive soon to dig her from the rubble.

"Help!" she screamed, the loudest yet. And then something grabbed her exposed foot. It was a human hand or hands. She yelped like a dog. And like a dog, she was totally reliant on this human. "Please, get me out of here!"

The hand continued to grope her foot, fondling her toes in a very titillating way, sticking its fingers between her toes, and petting her foot like the top of a dog's head. Helen didn't get the inappropriateness of the actions, just that this person was her savior. When the hand stopped petting, it began digging her out. Little by little, she saw more and more light until she saw the very familiar face of a man in his fifties. He wasn't the principal of the school or even a teacher. How did she know him?

"Give me your hand." He pulled her upright, and she tried to maintain her balance on the rubble.

Helen surveyed the scenery, and another layer of confusion consumed her. They were standing in a large hole—a deep hole half the size of a football field. The walls were dirt, and the bottom was filled with all kinds of trash: appliances, furniture, wood, tires, and bags of rotting food waste. Now she understood why it smelled so bad.

"Oh my God, a little girl?" a voice from behind shrieked.

Helen turned to see a woman with hair so bleached it almost glowed—at least the parts that weren't brown with mud or possibly shit.

"I'm not little," she stated, as one of her pet peeves was being treated like a child by her grandparents. "Where are we? What's going on?"

The man frowned. "We've been dumped in a landfill, it seems. Like pieces of trash."

THE WEATHERMAN

"You're bleeding," the man told Helen.

She looked at her blood-covered hand, amazed a little finger prick could drain so much out of her. She wiped it on her already stained jeans. But that wasn't her only blood source - her entire left arm was also drenched.

"Oh, shit!" she cried, panic-stricken, as she felt for the injury causing the blood flood.

"Here." The man pulled a blood-stained towel out of the back pocket of his khakis and soaked the blood off her arm. He wasn't the gentlest of cleaners.

"Ouch!"

The bleached blonde stood next to them, her bottom lip quivering. "Oh, you poor girl. What monster would do this to a child?"

"Look, I'm not a child! Call me that again, and I'll kick your ass!" The woman's verging tears quickly dried. "What is going on? Why are we here?" Helen asked, still debating if they were standing in school-building debris.

"We don't know what's going on. We both woke up here, like you."

A scream erupted in the distance.

The man handed the blonde the towel. "Here, you help this small, bloody child."

Helen shot him a murderous look, which he appeared to ignore.

He began his treacherous journey through the stinking trash.

◎   ◎   ◎

Glen's phone alarm played the "Sounds of the Island" ringtone as he rolled over and reached for it, accidentally knocking it off the nightstand. It was three in the morning—his usual wake-up time to get to the studio by four. Hair and makeup were typically completed by five, followed by analysis and preparation for his weather reporting as the WLBV Action News meteorologist.

"Glen, what are you doing?" his wife asked, awake and annoyed.

"Sorry, honey." He slid out of bed and grabbed the phone on his way to the bathroom.

He checked himself in the mirror and groaned, feeling and looking older than he wanted at age fifty-five. The three glasses of scotch the night before hadn't helped, nor had the pack-a-day cigarette habit. He was determined to quit the smoking. The scotch, not so much.

"Extra concealer, please. I'm looking like I've had silicone implants under my eyes," Glen instructed the makeup woman at the station.

"Oh, don't be silly. You're as handsome as ever."

"Yeah, not as handsome as I was twenty years ago when I started this job." He wasn't sure how he'd lasted that long at one station. It wasn't unusual for a broadcast news outfit to rotate newscasters and supporting players, like the sports and weather reporters. He was a well-known celebrity in Shady Springs, Illinois, a neighboring city of Chicago but a fraction of the size: a small city with big-city sensibilities. Besides its own news and media station, it had a baseball and a hockey team, both minor league but respected.

Shady Springs also had an old, abandoned landfill.

"And I will remind you once more to take your umbrella with you this afternoon. At least until two, when the clouds should clear and the sun will make an appearance."

Glen concluded his noon weather reporting as the camera cut to the lead female news anchor. As he stood like a mannequin waiting for the off-the-air signal, Glen realized his lust for life at the studio was limp. He had been going through the motions for some time, bored out of his mind. The technological advances in weather tracking and reporting kept things a little interesting, but, ultimately, he sought outside sources for excitement. These outside sources were women and the occasional young girl.

"And we're wrapped!" a studio assistant yelled after the anchors said their goodbyes.

A young, attractive female production assistant approached Glen as everyone scurried from the set. "Are you turned off?" she asked, referring to his microphone.

"No. I'm turned on. I am totally turned on right now." She giggled and swatted his arm as he pulled his wire out from under his shirt and gave her his mini microphone. "My vehicle. One-thirty. It's unlocked."

"Are we ever gonna go anywhere respectable? Like a motel?" she asked as Glen laughed.

"Yeah, that's respectable. Back seat. I'll be sitting. You'll be straddling. One-thirty." He walked away from her and went to the control room to study the upcoming weather patterns and to hang out until the noon news.

At one twenty-five, he stepped into the elevator and pulled out a cigarette. As the door closed, he lit it and enjoyed a couple of drags, not really caring about the no-smoking policy. When the elevator opened to the parking garage, he was greeted by a young couple. They coughed and waved their hands in the air to clear the cigarette smoke. He chuckled and rushed to his SUV, eager to have sex with the twenty-two-year-old who looked twelve. He'd been married for thirty-five years, and infidelity was a way of life. Especially with his celebrity status. The young girls threw themselves at him, and he was weak.

"Hey there, you sexy beast," he heard as he arrived at his vehicle, but these words didn't come from the mouth of the hot production assistant. A frail, elderly woman appeared from the shadows, her gray hair pulled back in a bun, her wrinkled mouth shining with bright red lipstick. She was wearing a tight, short dress that nearly exposed her breasts, which sagged down to her belly. Glen imagined the production assistant could look like this in her geriatric years, but he knew he wasn't time-traveling.

"Um, hello." He scanned her from head to toe and began laughing hysterically.

"What's funny, sonny? You ain't never fucked an old gal before?"

"What?" Glen continued to laugh, looking around the garage. "What is going on? Is there a hidden camera somewhere?"

"I'm not your type, am I? You like the young'uns, don't you, sonny? The young'uns. The young, young, young—"

"Stop!" Glen yelled, no longer thinking any of it was funny. "Look, are you someone's grandmother? I mean, probably great-grandmother, right? I assure you, whatever you were told is a lie."

"Can we go inside?" She ran her hand over the hood of his vehicle seductively and then pulled her hand away and inspected her palm. "Shit, man. Don't you ever wash this son of a bitch?"

Glen felt a pinch to the right of his spine, and everything went black.

◎   ◎   ◎

"Help!" a voice screamed.

Glen lost his balance and fell face-first into a shallow soup of garbage vomit. He got himself up quickly and regained his balance, but he almost added his own vomit to the mix.

"I'm almost there!" he yelled, annoyed. As he wiped the slime from his face, a figure emerged from the trash to his right, startling him. This was not who was screaming for help.

"Holy shit. Are you alright?" Glen asked the person who appeared to be a man under the slime.

"What's happening?" the man asked with a soft-spoken voice.

"Clean yourself off. I'll be right back."

Glen continued to the victim in distress. This voice was female. He approached a mostly flattened hunk of metal resembling a large, crumpled piece of paper. It could've been a dryer when it was alive.

It started moving.

He carefully lifted it and pushed it aside, uncovering some pieces of shag carpet and a few small bags of trash, but no screaming woman. He continued to dig until a face appeared. The face was blackened with sludge from the bottom of the hole. She extended her hand, and he pulled her out. He asked if she was okay, besides the obvious, and she appeared to move without pain as she stepped out of her trash casket. He also caught her up to speed on where he suspected they were, which was obvious to her.

"I'm Glen, by the way. You may know me as the meteorologist on Channel five?"

"No. I don't."

"Oh. Okay. Well, let's find something to get you cleaned up. You're very black with dirt or sludge."

"No. I'm very black with black because I'm black," she corrected.

"Oops. Awkward." He nervously chuckled as they navigated through the debris to find a flat surface. They came to the man, still standing in the same spot, seemingly afraid to move.

"Are you sliced anywhere? Any blood?"

The man, still a bit in shock, looked himself over. "I don't think so."

Glen motioned for him to join him and the woman on their march to the center of the hole where the ground was less populated. This was where the girl and the blonde woman stood.

When they got to the flat ground, there was a silent pause as they all stood in a circle and stared. They stared at the surrounding mess. They stared at one another. They stared at themselves. Not one of them had any idea why or how they arrived in their disgusting new home, nor had they any idea what to do to flee it.

Also, they didn't realize four more people were buried around them.

One of these four was already dead.

THE BLONDE

M iranda worked at Nails and Nips, a manicure and pedicure beauty salon in Shady Springs. This was a low-stress follow-up to the banking job she'd worked at for five years until she attempted to kill her boss.

Miranda's time of abduction (TOA) arrived during a typical day. She spent the first hour of the morning yelling and threatening her three sons. Like most children, motivation to ready themselves for school was nonexistent, and unlike Helen's school district, they still had a full week of classes remaining before summer break. Miranda dreaded this break, for it was sometimes impossible to find babysitters for the kids during her work shifts. The ages of the children ranged from six to eleven—too young to leave alone—and getting her bitch of a mother to help was like clearing toe fungus from a gnarly customer's digit. Their father had left the family six months ago after he discovered Mommy was sleeping with her boss at the bank. This abandonment forced Miranda to move the kids into a tiny, two-bedroom apartment she could afford. Three children shared one room, and she had occasional guilt about that because her bedroom was big enough to share, but she needed the break from them at night.

"Will you stop your goddamn whining and put your shirt on?" she told the youngest, after his older brother smacked him upside the head.

"Why do you always stick up for Scott?"

"Because he's not a big baby like you!"

While never physically harming the boys, Miranda would verbally abuse them to get them to do what was required. Shame and guilt were her parenting tools. She'd left the physical disciplinary actions to her husband until she realized he was a disciplinary slacker. A year earlier, the school bus driver had delivered the middle boy to the front door, claiming he'd punched another boy, giving him a bloody nose. Miranda screamed at her husband to do something with the kid, as she was sick of his crap. He was escorted to his bedroom, and the door was closed. A minute later, screams and sounds of a belt slapping an ass were heard through the door. The other boys sat nervously and stared at their mother, who nodded and smirked with approval, until she heard the screeching of a piece of audio equipment gone bad. She hurried to the room and flung open the door to find her husband ripping a cassette tape out of the old tape player as her son sat on the bed, unscathed. Turned out they had a recording of screaming and crying and belt whipping. Each child had their own tape. When Miranda stepped out of the bedroom and peered at the other two boys, they were now the ones smirking, knowing what was really happening in that room.

Her husband was extremely bitter over the affair and refused to help with the kids—his way of getting back at her—although he did hint that he might be around soon to visit with them.

The school bus was outside, horn blowing. Miranda looked out the window.

"That asshole's early!" she muttered as she ran to the door and motioned for the driver to wait. "Okay, let's go, let's go! I can't drive you to school!"

She herded them like a collie gathering sheep, although she was far from the beauty of the collie. They moaned as they rushed out the door with their shoes untied, shirts untucked, and hair sticking out everywhere. She slammed the door behind them and sighed before walking to the kitchen and invading a cabinet for a bottle of ibuprofen. She threw a few pills in her mouth and walked to the refrigerator for a beverage, only to find all the children's lunch bags sitting on the top shelf.

"Oh my God!" she screamed as she grabbed one bag and threw it across the room. The bag split in mid-flight, and upon impact, a chocolate pudding cup exploded all over the sky-blue wall. The dark brown provided a pleasant contrast, almost turning the wall into an abstract piece of art, but Miranda didn't see it that way as she sat at the table and cried. She wanted to do well for her children, to be a good mother, so any time she sensed failure, she exploded. Thankfully, these explosions only happened when she was alone.

A knock at the door halted her tears. She assumed it was the neighbor coming to yell at her for the noise and the pudding catastrophe. She looked through the peephole and saw the top of someone's head. Gray hair. This wasn't her neighbor. She opened the door to greet a little old lady who tried to pull a pamphlet from her purse.

"Hello, miss. I was wondering—"

"Aren't you a little old to be selling the Mormon religion?" Miranda asked. She suspected this was the reason for the intrusion. At least once a week someone knocked, but it was usually a young, cute boy.

"Oh no, miss. I want to—"

"I'm going to be late for work." Miranda quickly closed the door on the old woman and grabbed a dishrag to clean up her pudding mess.

Another knock at the door.

"Go away, lady! Mormons are freaks!" she yelled.

Another knock.

She continued to clean, ignoring three more sets of knocks. In all her thirty-five years, Miranda refused to be a participant in organized religion. She prayed well enough on her own without direction from a holy figure.

The knocks finally ceased, and she continued her daily routine of preparing for work.

◉   ◉   ◉

"Oh, honey, I didn't need that glass of wine to drop my panties!" Miranda's client, Anisha, told her an hour later as she was digging jam from her toenails. "That boy had me at *hello*!"

Miranda laughed, wondering why the act of beautifying toes or fingernails prompted therapy sessions. And why wasn't she paid better tips for this service? The amount of gunk she was digging from Anisha's toes warranted a huge tip.

"Any time I get a *hello* it's from someone trying to get me to go Mormon."

"You know the old saying: once you go Mormon, you don't go … oh, shit. There is no saying about that. Just stay away from it, girl. Stay far away from that noise," Anisha warned.

Miranda laughed and continued to share her hectic morning and the story of the forgotten lunches. Anisha reassured her she was a great mother. Perhaps this reassurance was her extra tip.

After coloring Anisha's toenails metallic purple and sending her on her way, Miranda took a couple bags of trash out the back door down the alley. After tossing the bags, a familiar face appeared from around the corner of the building.

It was that old Mormon bitch!

"You have got to be kidding me! You followed me to my work?" Miranda asked as they got closer to one another. "I am not interested! And if you don't leave me—"

She heard a rustling behind her before she blacked out.

◘　　◘　　◘

Back in the landfill, Miranda was jolted out of her flashback by an enormous snake climbing her bare leg. She screamed and shook it off and ran as well as possible, eventually tripping over trash and falling into a small puddle of muck. The entire floor of the landfill wasn't completely flooded, but puddles of varying sizes existed throughout the uneven ground. It was possible to avoid those mini cesspools when you weren't running for your life.

"Gimme your hand," Helen said as she helped the woman to her feet. Miranda thanked the girl, happy to discover she wasn't all rough and tumble.

"Fucking snake! Did you see it? Oh my God!" Miranda shrieked, wiping her eyes. "I fucking hate snakes!"

Having owned several snakes during her brief life, Helen couldn't agree with this, but decided it wasn't an appropriate time to divulge that information. She spotted something peculiar. "Look!"

An arm was sticking out of a metal barrel, turned on its side about twelve feet away. They carefully made their way to it, Helen the first to arrive. She squatted and looked inside. "It's a body. A man."

Glen and the other two living sewer rats joined them. Glen pushed his way in front of Helen and motioned for the other man to assist him.

"What's your name?" Glen asked the man who'd somehow cleaned his face, exposing a chiseled jaw and a pointed nose. His hazel eyes emitted a slight glow.

"Colin."

"Colin, help me roll this out."

The barrel was a little buried, and it would be difficult to remove the body in the current location, so they rolled it over two smaller stacks of debris and came to a stop on the flat ground. Glen reached in and grabbed the man from under his arms as Colin kept the barrel from moving. He pulled the man completely out and rested him on the ground. He appeared dead.

"No!" the dead man screamed as he rolled onto his knees and tried to crawl away from Glen. "Don't touch me! Whoever you are, stay the hell away from me." The man was at least sixty and wore a black robe with a square of white in the front of his collar. He appeared to be a priest—a priest naked under his robe, his bare, dirty ass greeting the group as he crawled another couple of feet before stopping and looking up into the sky, continuing to plead with Glen.

This man of God was as blind as a bat.

THE PRIEST

Everyone gathered around the man who hatched from the barrel.

"Who are you heathens, and why have you abducted me?" he asked as he looked around, not making eye contact with anyone. His eyes had a blueish film over them, but the dark pupils were still visible.

"We haven't abducted you, Monsignor," Miranda said.

"Monsignor? I don't work at the Vatican. I'm a priest, for crying out loud." He tried to stand on his wobbly knees. Colin helped him up and pulled his robe down over his fully exposed penis. The priest was going commando.

"What do you plan to do with me? I have nothing, you know. You'll get nothing from me."

"Look, Priest, we all just showed up here. Nobody knows why," Glen said.

"Where is here?"

"What's it look like?" Miranda asked.

"It looks like night. Smells like death but looks like blackness. A black you could only understand if you were blind, like me."

"Shit! You're blind?" Miranda said and then felt stupid for cursing in front of a man of God, although she would've said a lot worse if he'd been a Mormon.

"Really? I totally knew by the way he was looking up in the air, and his eyes are freaky," Helen said, as Miranda shook her head and shushed her.

"That's what I was afraid of: freaky eyes. I asked Sister Theresa to let me know when they started looking bad. There is a procedure where they can remove my rotten eyes and replace them with fake, real-looking eyeballs. I thought it would be cool to pop out a fake one during mass or during a dull confession, just to be funny."

Helen laughed and thought that would be cool. The rest of the group looked at one another, not sure what to make of the comment.

"I'm Father Daniel, by the way. How many of you are there?"

They took turns announcing themselves, ending with Mia, the one who was black with black because she was black.

"No way! Mia Philly? From *Aces of Slade*?" Helen asked with excitement. *Aces of Slade* was a sitcom on the cable station, Young Kids Network.

"Yes." Mia shook her head and smiled at the acknowledgment. Being recognized by adoring fans never got old, even when she had rotten cabbage attached like Velcro to her short hair.

"I loved that show when I was younger. Until I realized it was cheesier than *Full House*."

Mia's smile disappeared. "It's only been on two seasons. And you're young right now. I don't get it."

"Please don't call her young, munchkin, shrimp, or little, like Orphan Annie. She'll punch your lights right out of your pretty little head," Glen cautioned.

"This is absolutely bonkers," Father Daniel interrupted. "How did this happen? Oh, wait, lemme think. The last thing I remember … I was up early. I had a special engagement at the church. Yes. I was hearing the confession of a dying woman."

◉   ◉   ◉

Father Daniel walked from the rectory to the church. It was seven in the morning, and he wished he was in his bed. He'd received a request to hear a confession. Although confessions were held on Saturday mornings, he made exceptions in special cases like this one. Time was of the essence: the woman making the confession was dying.

The path from the parish housing to the church was roughly twenty yards, and he handled this trek fine without his walking wand. He knew the path well, having been the priest at Holy Mary Parish for eight years. He prided himself on being self-sufficient, since a rare degenerative eye disease had robbed him of his vision five years earlier. The inevitability of his blindness allowed him to prepare. He learned Braille, set little markers around the rectory for guidance, and had special keys made in different shapes to know which fit the proper hole.

People constantly asked him how he kept the faith during and after losing his eyesight, and he mouthed the correct answer: it was God's plan for him and that he wouldn't be dealt that hand if God didn't think he could handle it. He became accustomed to sharing these thoughts, and it became easier through the years to lie. He'd made a career out of it. He wasn't entirely convinced God even existed. He'd had no special conversations with the supposed man above. No spiritual awakening or calling.

Few people knew of his acting background, and little evidence of it existed. He'd spent two years in New York City auditioning for stage and film, landing a couple of Broadway shows in ensembles, with enough pay to buy a few decent meals. He also did a few industrial videos and background work on television. Two of the three aspiring actors he shared an apartment with in Brooklyn found moderate success. Their successes stirred jealousy and bitterness in Daniel, which directed him to the coping mechanisms named drugs and alcohol. When he tired of that life, he went home to Illinois and to the safety of his religious-fanatic parents who encouraged him to seek a pure life. Preaching and acting on the church stage would keep him sober and satisfy the need to perform in front of an audience every week. And he would get free room and board and some money to do this—a complete no-brainer in Daniel's bible. He stuck mostly to the rules as a Catholic priest although he occasionally revisited alcohol and sex. In the end, it was all about appearances, and he made good on those, keeping indiscretions discreet.

When he stood up on that stage and delivered his sermons, he considered himself the Daniel Day-Lewis of Catholic priests.

"Do you need my assistance, Father?" Sister Theresa scared the crap out of him. Somehow, she had made it into the church without him knowing it. The door had been locked when he inserted his key.

"Sister, how did you get in here?"

"The back door. Sorry to have startled you."

Sister Theresa was in her forties. A newer and younger member of the clergy, who Father Daniel wanted to get to know on a more intimate level. He was slowly working up to that. It was still the *feeling out* stage of that conquest. He'd had a couple of trysts with nuns over the years, but they always progressed slowly. He threw the line out and waited for them to bite. It took time to be sure they wouldn't go Glenn Close and boil his bunnies or destroy his career.

"If you would like to show Loretta to the booth, that would be great, thank you." Loretta was the name the elderly woman had given when she phoned. She claimed to have incurable breast cancer with only weeks to live.

Father Daniel stepped into his side of the confessional booth and awaited Loretta.

"Hi, Father Daniel," a voice greeted from the other side of the booth. The two sides were separated by a wall with little holes, like a pegboard, so voices could be understood.

"Excuse me? Who are you?"

"Loretta."

"Oh, okay. How'd you sneak in?" Father laughed anxiously. "The doors were locked."

"The back. I snuck in behind that nun."

"Okay then, Loretta. Let us begin."

"Can you excuse the nun? I really want it to be just the two of us, Father Daniel."

Daniel appeased, exiting the room for a moment and dismissing Sister Theresa. When he returned, the old woman was crying on the other side of the wall.

"I'm sorry, Loretta, can I help you? Or do you wish to proceed with your confession?" Daniel asked.

"I'll confess if you confess, Father Daniel."

"Excuse me?"

"Confession. Do you ever confess to anyone, Father? I know you hear confessions, but do you ever confess your sins to anyone?" The old woman's tone changed. She switched from vulnerable and distraught to judgmental and evil, with a bitter twang.

"I thought you wanted me to hear your dying confessions, Loretta. Isn't that why I agreed to meet you today?" Daniel tried to take this conversation in the direction it was meant to travel. Perhaps the old woman was not in her right mind, her sickness taking over her body.

"Bless you, Father, for you have sinned. It's been never since your last confession. Your sins include sexual misconduct with the nuns, lying, cheating and stealing from this parish, and nonbelief in the higher power you claim to love and respect and preach. Your penance shall be five thousand Hail Marys and ten thousand Our Fathers." Loretta started laughing.

"Okay, look. What is this? I don't have time for bullshit."

"Oops. Add cursing to your list of sins, Father Daniel. That'll be ten more Our Fathers, please."

"Please leave this confessional at once," Daniel ordered.

Loretta started crying again. "I'm sorry, Father Daniel. I am not well. Can you please help me out of here? I don't think I can move my diseased legs." Loretta wailed now.

Daniel felt terrible for cursing at this poor, dying woman. But how had she known his sins? He left his side of the confessional and entered her side. As he kneeled to assist her, he felt a pinch in his back. His immediate thought was that his back had gone out again, so he paused for the pain to begin. Instead of throbbing discomfort, he became lightheaded and blacked out.

◙   ◙   ◙

"What did this old woman look like?" Glen asked.

"Helen Mirren, I imagined. I always put a voice with a recognizable face. Usually that of an actor. It's kind of a game I play."

"Shit. Sorry. I've never been around a blind person. I'll try to remember," Glen said, feeling slightly asinine. "The reason I asked was I also had an encounter with an old woman. I'm pretty sure that was the last thing I remember."

Everyone confirmed that they'd stumbled upon an elderly woman and that she was one of their final recollections before appearing in the burrow of filth. As they shared their stories, they didn't see the bulldozer slowly creeping toward the far end of the mouth of the landfill, preparing to add trash and to increase their discomfort.

THE ACTRESS

"Oh my God!"

The attention of the group turned toward Colin's outstretched hand, pointing to the bulldozer as it dumped a load of building waste from its bucket. Glen ran toward it, waving his hands as patches of shingles and bricks hit the bottom, stirring a cloud of dust.

"Help!" Glen screamed, his arms flapping so hard he would've taken flight if he'd been a bird.

"What is it? What's happening?" asked Father Daniel.

He was ignored as everyone trekked to the other end of the landfill, hoping whoever operated the tractor was going to rescue them. If this were a typical landfill, they'd be able to walk out without a problem, as the slopes weren't steep. This landfill had been altered; the slopes transformed into walls. The height of these dirt walls was roughly fifty feet—about the size of a five-story building. This huge hole in the ground now seemed to exist for illegally purging trash, both material and human.

By the time they reached the other side, after falling many times, the tractor had backed out of sight. The vehicle was too high out of the ground to identify the operator, and the raised bucket obstructed the view.

"Why didn't they stop? Surely, they saw us?" asked Mia.

Growing up in a large family, being seen and noticed was a struggle for Mia. The youngest of six children. By the time she popped out, it seemed her parents were over being parents. She guessed she'd been an accident since a six-year gap existed between her and her next youngest sibling. Mia was essentially raised by her older siblings while her parents began the second phase of their lives, becoming career-driven social butterflies once again.

Mia learned at a young age that performing at school was great for getting the attention she was missing at home. Although she wasn't the most convincing actress in her high school, she had the beauty of a star. She turned heads. This led to a local agent in Chicago by age fifteen and many commercial and modeling jobs in the years leading up to her move to California after she disappointed her parents by dropping out of college.

Finding an agent in Los Angeles proved difficult. The competition was fierce. She didn't stand out so much in this city, as everyone there was equally, if not more, beautiful. The year of college was not kind to her body, as she stress-ate away her unhappiness of being forced into schooling. Potential agents told her she needed to drop ten pounds, and she did so quickly by starving herself. Then she was told that her nose was too big and that this would prevent her from being leading-lady material. Hearing this from multiple agents deflated her nineteen-year-old self-esteem and forced her into plastic surgery. She had a large savings account with her modeling and commercial money from years ago and funded a nose job. She returned to one agent after her nose healed.

"Wow, Mia, your nose looks amazing!" the older woman told her. "But has anyone suggested you get a breast enlargement?"

"No." Mia was flabbergasted but tried to hide any type of reaction.

"Yeah, I'm sorry, hon. That should be your next step. You're rather flat chested."

"But I can pad myself."

"What are you going to do for a nude scene? You think they can CGI bigger tits?"

Frustrated, Mia stood and paced the room, biting her lower lip, unable to come up with any other suggestions to get her body green-lit.

"You think they can CGI a nicer version of you?" Mia spouted, and instantly regretted shooting the bullet.

"Do you know how many girls are out there with talent and nicer tits? You're a dime a dozen, hon. You've given me no reason to take a chance on you. Your resume is shit."

"I'm sorry. Look, how about I get a boob job and come back?"

The phone beeped, and the receptionist spoke on the intercom, "Lauren Tristen is here."

"Great, send her in."

"So can I come back?"

"Tristan has tits and a resume. She also has a gentle disposition and doesn't disrespect someone who holds the keys to her future. So, no. I don't want you back here. You are dismissed."

Mia walked to the door, defeated. She paused and turned back. "You're a failed actress, aren't you? You made nothing of yourself. That's why you're sitting behind that desk criticizing and being the bitter bitch that you are." Mia shot bullet number two—the bullet of death.

The agent stood and pointed to the door. "Get out of here. I'll make sure you never work in this town."

"Yeah, right. Your ego might believe that, but trust me, you're not that powerful."

Mia stepped out and closed the door behind her. As she walked to the elevator, she was followed by a man in a suit and tie. He entered the elevator with her.

"Did you sign with them?" he asked.

"Who are you?"

"I'm Bob with Hasbred Talent." Hasbred was the second largest talent agency in Los Angeles.

Mia smiled and shook his hand as the gray clouds cleared. "Nice to meet you, Bob. No. I did not sign with them. They're ass—I mean, um, I'm weighing other options right now."

Bob pulled a business card out of his pocket and handed it to her. Apparently, it was normal for competing talent agents to go undercover to recruit or steal talent. She looked down at the card, her eyes bypassing the small bosom that Bob wasn't asking her to enlarge.

"Please come see us. We'd love to have you do some readings for us, and then, perhaps, we can talk about representation."

"Can I come right now?"

Two months later, she was on the set of *Aces of Slade*, the situational comedy about the Aces family moving into the racist, fictitious town of Slade. She landed the lead role, although the circumstances leading up to it were never discussed with friends or family. It would be foolish to disclose her misdeeds.

◉   ◉   ◉

A few days ago, she'd returned to Shady Springs for her mother's birthday and took the afternoon to relax at the local park. The house was full of siblings and children, and she was getting a headache. Even though she was a semi-famous actor, she was still the forgotten daughter when the entire family gathered.

She wore a large straw cap and shades to remain anonymous while sitting on the park bench feeding the ducks pieces of Italian bread from her mother's birthday luncheon. The ducks became greedy, moving in closer and screaming for more.

"Okay, okay, settle down."

One overzealous mallard jumped into her lap, pecking violently for more bread. Mia screamed and pushed it away, her hat falling behind the bench.

"You shouldn't feed the ducks bread, you know, girlfriend." A frail old woman appeared from behind the bench, holding the straw cap. Mia smiled at her use of the term *girlfriend.*

"Oh?"

"It's not at all nutritious, you know. It makes their wings deformed, and they can't fly away from predators."

"Okay, duly noted, Grandma!" Mia chuckled.

The woman put Mia's straw hat on her head and strutted back and forth in front of her like a runway model. That "I'm Too Sexy" song filled Mia's head as she smiled and looked around the oddly deserted park, wondering if anyone else was witnessing this odd scene.

"I ain't yo grandmama!" the old woman said, trying to be all gangster.

"Okay, and I'm not your girlfriend. So we're even, I guess." Mia continued to smile, amused for the moment but slightly concerned she wouldn't get the hat back. It looked cheap, but it had a price tag of two hundred bucks.

"You shouldn't treat animals the way you treat your fellow actors," the lady warned.

Mia's smile disappeared, much like the ducks when the bread ran out. "Excuse me?"

Suddenly, Mia's shadow in front of the bench was overtaken by a much larger shadow. Someone had stepped up behind her, but before she could turn around, she became much like the combined shadows: black and inanimate.

◎　　◎　　◎

"That sounds like my lady, Loretta," Father Daniel said after he and the others had listened to Mia's story. "And what did she mean about treating your fellow actors bad?"

"I don't know what that crazy lady was talking about," Mia lied. She knew exactly what she meant, but that was not the business of the others.

When the others told their stories, they intentionally left out their incriminating conversations with the lady, but they had anxiety over her knowledge of their lives, mainly of their wrongdoings.

"Okay. We've established we were abducted by this old woman and that she must have had help, but this knowledge isn't getting us out of here. Anyone have any ideas?" Glen asked, prompting them to scan the landfill and look up at the opening. They had all been stripped of belts and phones before being thrown into the hole.

"Can we make a huge stack of trash and climb up?"

"What if we find materials to make a pole or extended rope we can throw up?"

"And attach to what?"

"What if we make a human ladder? Climb up each other's backs?"

"Still wouldn't be tall enough."

Their escape plan was disrupted by a scream. A woman was attempting to emerge from an unvisited corner of the hole. Colin quickly jumped through the trash to get to the woman who had a large cut across her forehead. The bleeding had stopped, but there was dirt mixed in the gash. Ripe for infection.

"Where's the old lady?" the woman asked once Colin had her on her feet. "Where is she? She has my fucking daughter!"

"She's not here."

The woman fell back onto a broken wooden pallet and started crying.

"Look, everything's going to be fine," Colin said. "We're working on a way out right now. Come on, let's get out of here and over to the others." He helped her up, and they slowly made their way back to the dry center of the landfill.

"I'm Punam. And I'm an alcoholic." She looked around with confused, glazed eyes, hugged herself, and lowered her head, a great sadness overtaking her.

"Punam, that's a pretty name," said Miranda, trying to cheer her up a bit.

"Don't humor me. Get me a fucking shot. Wild Turkey," Punam demanded in her Native American accent.

They all looked at her with concern. She had lost a lot of blood from her head wound and from a deep back laceration that hadn't been spotted by the others. They knew something was wrong.

Glen walked over to her with his hand extended, pretending to hold a glass. "You're a lady after my own heart. I love a good bourbon. Here you go." She swatted his hand away. "Okay, fine. Be that way."

"Here, sit down." Colin pulled a slightly mangled office chair from the trash. He helped her into it.

"Thank you, handsome. Now, who do I have to blow to get a fucking drink?" Punam appeared to be in her late forties to early fifties and clearly had some issues with alcohol, which were manifesting from her current unhealthy state. "Get me a fucking drink!"

She grabbed Glen's crotch and squeezed. He screamed and slapped Punam upside her head, sending her flying back into the trash. She landed face-first, exposing her torn shirt and back injury. Colin helped her onto her butt and propped her up, but she was unconscious. Or dead.

"What is wrong with you?" Miranda asked Glen.

"She grabbed my nuts and squeezed. Really fucking hard!"

"You might've killed her!"

"She wasn't letting go! I had to do something. If you had balls, you'd understand." He sat on the ground and lay back, taking deep breaths to help ease his pain.

"Sounds like she's lost her mind," Father Daniel said.

"You think!" Glen shot back.

"She's still alive." Colin leaned her forward, ripped open the back of her shirt, and inspected her wound, which was deep and still bleeding. "She's lost a lot of blood and could go into hypovolemic shock." He received a couple of strange looks. One was from Father Daniel, but he was looking at Helen instead, and she was ten feet away from Colin.

"I'm a nurse," Colin said to a collective sigh of, "Oh."

"When a body loses twenty percent or more of blood or fluids, the heart can't pump or circulate the remaining blood effectively, which was why she was in a disoriented state. If we don't stop the bleeding or get her help soon, her organs will shut down, and she'll die."

"Shit. I thought she was turning into a zombie or something," Glen said.

"What is wrong with you? This is not a zombie apocalypse. You bitch-slapping her could've been it for her. She may never wake up!" Colin said.

"I'm sorry, but my fucking balls may never recover! And who's to say this isn't a zombie apocalypse?"

"Just shut up."

"We have to get out of here," Helen said. "Why can't we dig holes in the dirt wall, kind of like steps? Dig one and climb one. Dig another and climb another. Keep doing this? I'm the smallest. Wouldn't it be easiest for me to do?"

"That's a great idea, Helen," Mia said. "Come on."

Mia grabbed Helen's hand, and they made their way to the wall. The others watched, mostly doubting the plan had potential, but not wanting to destroy the girl's hope. The actress and the girl found a four-foot-long metal pipe and a splintered piece of wood and began digging the first step. The sun disappeared, and daylight turned to dusk as they completed two steps, roughly three feet apart. With Mia pushing and supporting Helen from behind, she put her feet inside the first hole in the wall—one bare foot and one with a ripped sneaker—and it held her weight. Helen then grabbed the ledge made from the second hole and froze. There was no way to move up. If she pulled herself up to the second hole, she couldn't balance herself to dig the next step. She had nothing to grab to steady herself.

"Not working?" Glen asked as he joined them.

"No. Any better ideas?"

An eerie howl sounded in the distance. Another followed. And another. Soon, a chorus of creepy, wild animal howls filled the air. Coyotes? Wolves? Did these creatures live in Illinois, and were they even in their home state? They did not know where the crater from hell was located or how long they had been unconscious. So many questions without answers.

The first night would be a long night.

THE NURSE

The digging in the dirt wall was suspended until morning, as nothing could be accomplished in the dark. They hoped to brainstorm a better idea before then. For now, they created dry, warm spaces in the center of the large trash bin, prepping the area for, hopefully, a little sleep. The temperature was dropping as it does in the spring: chilly nights turned into cold mornings. Disorientation had kept them from thinking too far ahead of the game earlier in the day. If their minds had been clearer, they would've built some sort of shelter. Instead, they used trash, such as plastic bags, flattened cardboard boxes, and various types of stained, smelly fabrics, to create a softer ground and to cover themselves.

The darkness and the quiet between the howls revealed their hunger as stomach churning increased. Glen joked that the different gurgles and groans played the theme to *Star Wars*. They'd search for anything edible tomorrow, but there wasn't much hope of food, unless something was protected from the environment in one of the trash bags. Canned goods, perhaps? Their complaints about hunger were few as they realized it wouldn't make a candy bar or a chicken leg appear.

"Shut the fuck up!" Glen screamed up at the howling beasts.

They seemed to surround the opening above, intermittently growling and howling. When they screamed in unison, it was as ear piercing as an ambulance siren. Father Daniel identified the howls as coyotes, as he'd encountered them on his yearly camping-for-faith retreats. This was a sign that they may still be in Illinois.

"How is Punam?" Glen asked Colin, who monitored her health. He'd never struck a woman and was bothered by it, but it'd been defensive. She was on the verge of destroying his manhood, which was his life.

"She's breathing."

"Do you think she'll be all right?"

"If we don't get help as soon as we can see in front of us tomorrow, she'll probably die."

Colin had witnessed this loss-of-blood shock before while pulling an all-nighter at the emergency room. Coincidentally enough, it was his TOA.

◎　　◎　　◎

Colin's boyfriend, Jack, had just moved into his small townhouse. Sharing his place with a male love interest was a first for Colin after coming out of his cobwebbed closet five years earlier at age thirty. Once they reached their two-year anniversary, Jack convinced Colin it was time to snuggle every day together under the same roof. Snuggling was tedious for Colin, but he agreed to the next step. This eliminated Jack's suggested opening up of the relationship, which Colin was not comfortable doing. He was conservative at heart.

After going on their first four dates and really connecting, they ended up in bed together for the first time, and after mild play, Jack disclosed he was HIV positive. Colin lay in bed, silently absorbing the increasingly common situation. Although he was well informed and trained on HIV and AIDS as a nurse, he had yet to encounter it on a personal level.

He felt the way Kevin McCallister did after he slapped aftershave on his face in *Home Alone*.

"Say something," Jack said. He explained he hated telling a male prospect he was positive because it always sent them running, that he had purposely waited to tell

Colin, for he'd seen him in gym shorts and sneakers and knew he could run fast. He admitted that hiding his status was a manipulative, but necessary game.

"What should I say, Jack? That I'm disappointed? That I wished you'd told me this on date number one?"

"Yes. Say that. Tell me everything you're feeling. But know that I really like you."

"We just exchanged fluids! You put me at risk!" Colin's voice rose as he sat up against his headboard and looked at Jack.

"Not really, Colin. I'm undetectable. I knew what we were doing was completely safe, or I wouldn't have done it."

"I understand undetectable, but nothing is ever 100 percent safe. You still should've told me, given me the option to proceed."

Jack sat up and climbed out of bed, his toned, slim body bending down to slide on his plaid boxers. "Would you have proceeded?"

"Hell no! Not this soon. Not until I knew if there was a future with you."

"Okay. Fair enough. I'm going to give you some space to decide if there is a future for us. I hope there is." Jack grabbed the rest of his clothing and left the bedroom. Colin did not stop him.

After a week of much thought and consideration, Colin continued with the relationship. He felt a connection with Jack that hadn't existed with other men, and he wanted to see where it took them. He proceeded with caution.

"You're staying in tonight, right?" Colin asked Jack as he threw on his scrubs, pre-TOA.

There was a huge rave happening that night, and Colin wasn't comfortable with Jack attending without him. Jack still enjoyed going to the bars, but Colin was a homebody. The difference caused tension. Colin compromised occasionally, but he was convinced healthy relationships did not include techno beats and flashing lights—too many opportunities for drunken, or ecstasy-fueled debauchery.

"Yeah. I'm going to jerk off to that new Ryan Reynolds film."

"Great. Remind me not to bring one of those black lights home soon."

Jack's sex drive was off the charts, which created another disconnect and was the reason Jack suggested the open relationship. Colin spent a lot of energy on the relationship and really loved Jack, but in the back of his mind, he wasn't convinced the couple would stand the test of time.

Colin kissed Jack goodbye and threw him a roll of paper towels on his way to the front door.

"I love you."

Colin stopped in his tracks, one foot out the door. It occurred to him he hadn't heard this proclamation of love for several weeks or months, even. He also hadn't said it in a while. Earlier in their relationship, they'd said it all the time.

"Back at you, freak." It was a playful response they took turns using, an idiosyncrasy of their coupling.

"*Benny and Joon* tomorrow?" Jack asked, another quirky couple tradition as they both loved the film starring Johnny Depp and Mary Stuart Masterson. After the fifth viewing together, they concluded the misunderstood love between the two characters resonated with them.

"Absolutely. I'll pick up some Sangria. Have a good night." Colin pulled the door closed and walked to the driveway. He tried not to read anything into Jack's sudden romanticism.

Half an hour later, he walked the ER floor, assisting the few patients in beds, the emergency room low key for a Friday night. Shady Springs Memorial Hospital was the leading medical destination within a thirty-mile radius. Colin thought he'd seen it all in his eighteen months of employment. He was wrong.

At two in the morning, ambulances began unloading victims of a shooting spree. Colin had been helping an old lady to the restroom—yes, *that* old lady—and hadn't heard the details of the attack until he got back to the admissions desk. It had happened at a gay club outside of Shady Springs. The club was named Bounce—the same bar hosting the rave. Colin was shocked by this news, but he was immediately thrust into lifesaving mode. In the back of his mind, he was relieved that he'd worked that night and Jack was safely at home.

"Colin?" a victim said as he wiped blood from his face. It was Jason, a mutual friend of the couple. He was more of Jack's buddy and often the instigator in getting Jack to go out, which annoyed Colin.

"Jason? You're going to be okay. Where are you hurt?" Colin always told incoming patients they would be okay, even if he knew their injuries were life-threatening. The least he could do was provide comfort for them in their final moments. He couldn't be that upbeat with the patient's family, though. When he discovered Jason had been shot multiple times in the stomach and chest, he knew the outlook was dire. A doctor arrived and cut Jason's shirt away, exposing the holes.

"I'm sorry," Jason said right before he lost consciousness.

Colin was puzzled over his apology until the next stretcher rolled into the ER two minutes later. Jack was on it, also covered in blood.

He spotted Colin. "Baby, help me. Help me. I'll never lie to you again. I swear to God."

Colin took a quick moment to process and to understand the situation. He'd been trained to put emotions aside, that lives depended on it, and this would be no exception. Another doctor arrived and removed Jack's shirt, exposing three gunshot wounds in Jack's chest. His eyes started fluttering wildly.

"He's hypovolemic!" the doctor shouted, followed by instructions for helping.

Colin failed to contain his emotions. He began sobbing uncontrollably. A nurse, who knew the couple well, pulled him away and directed him to an outside bench at the back of the building, away from the chaos. She assured him Jack would be fine and then ran back into the hospital. A lamp illuminated a shrub of common holly, and he stared hard at it, the leaves shiny and rigid. He thought of the previous Christmas, of how Jack had insisted on decorating with real holly and how it quickly died, the prickly leaves cutting his fingers as he cleaned them off the floor. Colin's anger for Jack's betrayal wrestled with his love for him and his fear of losing him. He wanted to go back inside to help but couldn't move.

He also knew why Jack was being so sweet to him before he left for work. He wished he would've read more into it and probed him about it.

"I'm sorry for your loss." The old lady from earlier stood in front of him.

He composed himself a bit. "No loss. Yet. But I'm afraid…." Colin cried again. This old woman reminded him of his grandmother who'd passed a few years earlier. He'd been very close with her and taken her loss hard. He hoped this stranger would hug him the way his grandmother used to.

"Are you aware that AIDS sickness was God's way of fixing his screw-up?" she asked as the warm, grandmotherly vibe vanished.

"What? What are you talking about?"

"Men in bed with each other is not natural. It just isn't. Something had to be done about that."

Colin was confused. Did she know about the shooting, or was she some homeless dementia patient from the third floor of the hospital?

Colin's eyes fluttered like Jack's, and he left the conscious world.

◎　　◎　　◎

Back in the black hole, Colin quietly cried in the darkness, thinking about Jack, not knowing if he was dead or alive and feeling anger towards his betrayal, which led to guilt for not being completely sympathetic. Also, not knowing the probable death toll in the shooting or who was responsible feasted on his brain. After the forty-nine deaths at Pulse nightclub in Orlando last year, Colin never wanted to enter another gay bar again. Jack had calmed his fears, though, convincing him not to let the terrorists win. And look what had happened.

Punam screamed and started convulsing, which transitioned Colin's somber state of being to one of alertness and heroics. He wrapped his arms around her and held her tightly, hoping this would calm her. After several minutes, she quieted and slipped off to sleep again. He feared her organs were shutting down. The only thing that would save her life was a blood transfusion. And quick. The likelihood of this happening was slim. She may not make it through the night. One saving grace was the chill in the hole. A fine layer of cold moisture clung to everything.

"I can't believe this is happening," Miranda said, a voice from the blackness. The sky was cloudy, which eliminated any moonlight or starlight. Their eyes were adjusted enough to make out dark gray movements or shadows, but that was the extent of their vision. They related to the blind priest.

"Allow your other senses to excel," Father Daniel instructed. "What do you smell? What do you feel? What do you hear? What do you taste?"

"I taste a turd," Helen said. "I feel like my breath smells like crap."

Father Daniel continued, "Use your other heightened senses to keep you alert in the night. For example, I smell a wood fire. The smoke from a burning log, which means there is a house or houses not too far from here. That's good to know."

"That's great, but I can't smell anything but this nasty shit all around us," Mia said.

"That's because your sense of smell is bulked into one big cloud of fragrance. It's weak, generalized. You can only separate multiple individual smells when you work at it or detach from your other senses. I've been doing it for years. Trust me, I know it's possible."

"That gives me a great idea—fire. If we can start a fire and signal help, that could be our way out," Glen suggested. "I can use my sense of touch right now to dig for objects to rub together to create that spark. I watch *Survivor*."

He slid out from his soggy cardboard box and cautiously walked away from the group in the center until he hit a pile of rubbish and carefully touched and pulled things. He found a couple pieces of wood and what felt like branches. And then he touched what felt like a sneaker. Shoestrings would be great for creating a friction spark. He grabbed the shoe, but it seemed to be wedged. It wasn't moving. He pulled harder this time, and then it moved, but not toward him. There was a shuffle in the trash pile in front of him, and then he was struck in the face by a fist. He grunted as he flew backward and landed on his ass.

"Oh my God. Oh my God! Fuck!" The voice came from a man emerging from the trash pile.

And then it began to downpour.

THE CONVICT

Byron had the itch, and ointment was not the cure. It was exactly eight months since he was released from a jail in Illinois where he'd been imprisoned for over a year. His sentence was five years, but good behavior and testimony against a sought-after Ohio drug lord with connections to a Mexican drug cartel led to a shortened sentence. He decided to stay in Illinois after his release and made his home in Shady Springs, as this was the home to a large halfway house where he took up residence until facilitators believed him capable of clean survival in the real world. Byron had a lengthy resume of crime, most of which he never got caught for, but the drug dealing caught up with him. He also had a nasty heroin addiction capped with regular cocaine and marijuana usage. Plus, he also ran over his former best friend, Vincent, in a supermarket parking lot while trying to elude the police. The emotional devastation over this accident motivated him to clean up his act. He eventually wanted to head back to Ohio to make things right with Vincent, and a phone call seemed a good place to start.

◙   ◙   ◙

"Hello?" Vincent answered, his voice sounding tired.

"Hey, buddy," Byron said.

There was a long pause. Byron gathered Vincent was trying to recognize his voice, knowing he'd lost some memory and mental functions because of the accident, an unfortunate circumstance of being in the wrong place at the wrong time.

"Byron?"

"It's me, buddy. Yes. How are you?"

"Aren't you still locked up?"

"No. I've been out for a few months."

"Damn. You weren't in long." Vincent's disappointed tone filled Byron's ear, and he knew the conversation would be strained.

"Look, Vinnie, I want to see you face to face. I want to explain things to you. I want to make things right again."

"That's not a good idea. Are you back?"

"Not yet."

"Where are you?"

"Illinois. Shady Springs."

"Hey, a town made for shady people. Makes sense you're there. Maybe the Springs will cleanse you, make you a better person." Byron had never connected the name of the city in that way and was a bit impressed with Vincent's quick wit.

"I'm going to make this better if it's the last thing I do, Vinnie. I swear to you. Once I get out of this halfway house, I'm coming to see you."

Silence.

"Vinnie?"

"I can't walk without a cane. I can't think too much about anything without getting an unbelievable fucking headache. I can't remember where I put the house keys. I can't match my clothes because I can't see certain colors, Byron. And it's all your fault. You swore to me when we moved to Ohio together that you would make something of yourself, that you wouldn't end up a loser like your dad and brother. You're worse than they ever were."

"I'm going to be better. My life will turn around. You'll see."

"I'll, see? You know what? I don't want to see. I don't care what happens to you. Leave me alone. Never call me again."

"Vinnie? Vinnie?" Dial tone. "Fuck!" Byron threw the phone across the TV room. It hit a vase of flowers, knocking it over and shattering it on the hardwood floor, water and glass and spring flowers flying everywhere.

Counselor Rich appeared in the doorway. "What's going on here?" He was a large African American man whose physical stature could scare the Terminator.

Byron cleaned the mess. "I'm sorry. I had a night terror." This was the same excuse Byron had given Rich a few nights ago when he kicked his roommate off his bed because of his snoring.

"It's the middle of the day."

"Oh yeah. A day terror then."

Byron kept cleaning as Rich watched for another minute and then left the doorway. Fifteen minutes later, Byron lit a cigarette in the fenced courtyard and thought about Vincent and their history together. He was the only person in his life who'd given him a second chance. And a third. For years, he was the best friend a guy could have—nurturing, forgiving, and thoughtful. Byron knew he could never get it all back, but even a tiny amount of forgiveness would fuel his recovery. He wasn't giving up the fight.

It was three thirty, and he needed to get ready for work soon. Flipping burgers at the fast-food joint down the street was his transitional gig. He hated it, but he maintained it as a way of getting out of the claustrophobic house and the room he shared with the smelly little person.

Fifteen people stayed at the house, and it was an honor system with rules and curfews. So far, Byron obeyed. But the itch to do something bad never completely went away, and the drug addictions were only quieted by the withdrawal meds. Even if he wanted them, he wouldn't know where to look for drugs in this new town.

"Aren't you late for work?" Leroy, his little roommate, asked from behind, startling him.

"Jesus! Don't you know how to make noise? Ya know, to signal you're coming?" Byron didn't like Leroy. He stunk.

"Have you seen me? I'm too small to make noise."

"Are you too small to shower too? I'm sick of sleeping in that fucking room with your odor. Fuck, I smell you out here even. You suck the fresh out of the air." Byron had talked to the counselors about this issue, and they had addressed it with Leroy.

"I have fish odor syndrome. How many times do I have to tell everyone? Aren't you late for work?"

Byron smashed his cigarette in the empty birdbath and tossed his butt over the fence. "I work at five."

"What did that old lady want?"

"What old lady?"

"She was sitting out here earlier. Somehow, she got into the backyard. I was out here jogging, and I almost ran into her." Leroy jogged around the yard to avoid people heckling him on the city streets. "She asked for you."

"I don't know anything about it. I have to shower for work. Wanna join me?" Byron passed Leroy and went inside.

Leroy followed. "Okay."

"I was fucking joking. Get away from me."

Byron showered, checked out at the front desk, and headed to Burgers and Buns. While waiting at a crosswalk, someone tugged at his navy polyester shirt. He turned to face an old lady.

"You got dope?" she asked him.

He laughed. "What?"

"I need some dope. You got some? How about heroin?"

Byron looked around, sure someone was playing a joke on him. Or testing him. "I ain't got shit, lady. What do you want with it, anyway?"

"I want a high. I have some if you want some. Come here." She grabbed his shirt again and pulled him down the side street.

"I thought you wanted some. Now you're saying you have some?"

She giggled as they turned another corner and entered an abandoned alley. "Have you run anyone over lately?"

"What the fuck are you—"

"Do you like Eagles?" she asked.

"Eagles? Why do you care if I fucking like eagles, lady?"

She started dancing in a circle, arms stretched into the air, singing lyrics to Life in the Fast Lane by The Eagles. Byron now understood the question. He watched her for a moment and decided she was a fruitcake and he needed to get away.

That was his last recollection of the day.

◎　　◎　　◎

Byron awoke to the tugging of his shoe, but even after lashing out and standing on a flat surface, he still could see nothing in the pitch dark.

"Did you have to punch me?" Glen asked the shadow being pummeled by rain, an unexpected and unwelcome gift from Mother Nature.

"This has to be a nightmare. Where's the old lady?" Byron asked to a collective sigh from the group, which informed him there were others. Glen pulled him over to the group as they quickly used trash to shield them from the rain. Glen explained to Byron that they had all been through similar experiences with the old lady and that they planned to get out of the landfill in the morning.

"I'm so cold," Helen said, shivering. Miranda wrapped her body around her and rubbed her arms. The temperature was in the high forties, but the rain chilled them to their bones.

"The trash bag had a hole in it, and you leaked something out all over the kitchen floor when you took the bag to the trash. You never cleaned it. Now the floor is sticky," Punam said, awake once again and still disoriented. The cold and the wetness stabilized her physical condition a bit.

"Punam. Can you hear me? What is your last name?" Colin asked, trying to gauge her confusion. The rain slowed a bit, but they were now all sitting in mud puddles.

"Shetty," she answered.

"Yeah, that's an understatement," Byron said.

"Shetty. Her last name is Shetty. Not shitty," Colin said. "How old are you? When were you born?"

"Why are you asking me these questions? Where am I?"

Colin explained everything to her as Byron also listened intently, his aggravation building.

"I can't just sit here and do nothing right now. This hole can't be that deep. I'm climbing out of here!" Byron stepped out from under the limp cardboard sheet Daniel and Miranda held and made his way to the start of the piles of rubbish. He carefully stepped up onto them and continued through, his movement becoming less and less audible until they no longer heard foot crunching.

"This guy is nuts," Glen said to the group.

"How many times do I have to tell you? Wild Turkey!" Punam returned to her hometown-named disorientation as Colin wrapped a wet sweater around her, hoping the cold and wet would delay the inevitable.

THE ALCOHOLIC

Byron reached the dirt wall without falling, although he did slice himself a few times as his jeans slid up his legs when his feet dipped into various-sized openings beneath the trashy surface. The darkness surrounding him added another element of treachery, but it helped not to see the vastness of the landfill or the height of the walls. It kept his determination strong.

He hit the wall head-on; the exterior layer of dirt had turned to mud thanks to the downpour and continued drizzle. He worked his hands into the wall a little, through the mud, but the next layer was hard and dry. He tried to climb the wall, using his hands and feet like an exercise machine at the gym, minus the hot chicks in spandex. This wasn't a totally ridiculous attempt to escape. He made it up about five feet until the dirt crumbled under his weight and he fell on his ass. The rain stopped, the clouds cleared, and a half-moon illuminated the landfill. As he stood and regained his balance, he could see the height of the walls. His determination fizzled.

Back at base camp, the group was relieved the shower ended. Even though it was a cold shower, it cleaned them up a bit, as they'd discover at dawn.

Punam lay still and quiet. Colin brushed her long black hair out of her eyes. His treatment of her as a patient was important to him since he'd been unable to complete the care for the shooting victims in the emergency room. His mind was always a thought away from that scene. And from Jack. Punam quickly sat up and grabbed Colin, who was kneeling over her, and pressed her lips against his. Her mouth tasted like liquor, cigarettes, and blue cheese, and Colin almost vomited once he detached from her. She fell back on her side.

◉　　◉　　◉

"What a crazy bitch!" the short, bald man said as he left the bar, shaking his head. He was talking about Punam, who had just called him a fuckface. In her defense, he had just attempted to shove his hand up her dress while they sat at the bar prior to her TOA.

"That was Charles. Don't mind him," the bartender told her.

"Um, excuse me, but I mind having his filthy hands up my dress," she shot back and then ordered another shot.

This was a new watering hole. She was booted from the last one down the street because she was frequently inebriated and obnoxious. Also, her husband told the bar owner to forbid her from entering. Punam's life had been wonderful and alcohol-free until two years ago.

She had met her future husband in law school and married him shortly after they both graduated. They became partners in their own family practice in Shady Springs and tried to have a family of their own. After several years of failed attempts, they finally succeeded.

And then the unspeakable happened: their one-year-old daughter disappeared without a trace. Punam and her husband were out on the town celebrating their anniversary, and when they returned to their home three hours later, the sixteen-year-old babysitter and their daughter were missing and hadn't been found since. This was the first time the couple had used a babysitting agency, and it received a five-star rating, but somehow this mentally unstable girl had passed all the prescreening tests. The police discovered she'd secretly gone off birth control pills, hoping to trap her boyfriend, who planned on dumping her. A baby never emerged, and the boyfriend left her a short while later. The police concluded she had convinced herself that the Shetty's child was hers and her ex-boyfriend's.

No law enforcement expert could explain how the girl and the baby had bypassed the amber alerts. This was a very calculated kidnapping, or the girl had been hiding nearby, possibly being assisted by a friend or family member.

Two years later, they weren't convinced their beautiful daughter was even still breathing. The thought of her death pushed Punam over the edge. She self-destructed as her husband focused on keeping their law firm running, taking on more cases and working them alone as Punam drowned herself in booze in dive bars. The dark, seedy drinking holes were easier to hide from the public. The news coverage from years ago still resonated, and she was still treated sympathetic by the public and the sad sentiments drove her crazy. The notoriety was unwelcomed and pushed her into further depression.

Her cell phone vibrated in her jeans, and she fished it out of her pocket. It was her husband.

"Yeah?" she answered, knowing what was coming.

"Can I pick you up, honey?" Gerald asked.

"One more drink, please. How was work?" She didn't really care, but this was the only conversation they ever really had. After the kidnapping of their daughter, their distress turned to bitterness and anger toward each other. Punam blamed Gerald for wanting to go out that evening, and Gerald blamed Punam for selecting the babysitting agency. He had a niece who had babysat before, but Punam didn't like her because she smoked.

Punam had been born in a large city in India named Hyderabad. Her father moved the family to the United States when she was five. She brought her native language of Telugu with her and maintained it throughout her thirty-six years of life as a second language to English. Whenever she felt like cursing or saying something shameful, she used Telugu. Gerald had been born and raised in Chicago, and the pairing of the two created much conflict between the families for racist and religious reasons.

"I need you back. We got a huge case, and I can't farm it out. Please consider getting help, Punam. You know I support you a hundred percent."

He had convinced her to get help several times before, and it worked temporarily. For a couple weeks or an entire month even, she remained clean, but something would always cause a relapse. She kept waiting for him to pull the plug. The uncertainty of the kidnapping kept them connected through dysfunction. She was legitimately bored with drinking, but it was an addiction she couldn't quit. Besides, it numbed the pain.

"Come get me in thirty minutes." She ended the call and set the phone on the bar. "Evaru miru oka paniyam pondadaniki ikkada cuttu vicu untundi?" she yelled to the bartender. He turned away from the baseball game on the television above the bar and approached her.

"What?"

"I said who do you have to blow around here to get a drink?"

He rolled his eyes and poured her another shot of Wild Turkey. She gulped it as her phone vibrated on the bar. It was an unlisted number.

"I don't want to upgrade my data package. You should upgrade your life. Get a fucking real job!" she yelled before she even heard a voice. She squinted to see the "end," button.

"I have your daughter," a female voice said.

Punam quickly put the phone back in her ear. "What did you just say?"

"I have your daughter."

"Who is this?" Her adrenaline rose, and those four little words had the impact of a collision of two inhabited planets. This was something she fantasized about. She dreamed of hearing those words.

"Come outside. Don't tell anyone. Meet me behind the bar." The phone went dead.

"Hello?" Punam dropped the phone, her trembling hand unable to keep a grasp. She grabbed it and clenched it, looking around the bar and taking a deep breath. Had this really happened, she wondered, as she hit a couple buttons on the phone and saw the unlisted number once again. Should she call Gerald? Would this person know she did and cause harm to her baby? Her head spun with the possibility of seeing her daughter and all that it entailed. It was also spinning because she was very drunk.

She stood up and shoved the phone into her pocket, totally disregarding the thought of calling her husband. She stumbled toward the door.

"Hey, lady! You didn't pay your bill!" the bartender yelled.

She waved him off, pushed open the big metal door, and slid onto the empty front patio area. She turned left and followed the sidewalk around the lit front to the dark side of the building and then to the dark backside of the bar. A security light above the back door shined on a small figure. Gray hair glistened above a wrinkled, old face.

"Who are you? Where's my baby?" Punam still considered her daughter a baby even though she was three years of age.

The old woman bent down and picked up a large potato sack. As Punam walked toward her, she pulled a body out of the bag by its leg. Two more steps toward the old woman and — blackout.

◎　　◎　　◎

Byron made it back to camp and shared his news. He'd been unsuccessful at climbing the wall, and they would have to wait until morning to attempt more escapes. Helen explained she had already tried the same thing as he sat with the rest of the group. Together they formed a perfect circle, except for the unconscious

Punam who was spread out off to the side. The Weatherman. The Girl. The Blonde. The Nurse. The Priest. The Actress. The Convict. The Alcoholic. Eight of them thrown into a trash grave. All of them losing memory after meeting the old lady who called herself Loretta. All of them had left out the final details of their stories: the bad things the old woman had smacked them with across their faces. But they all knew a deeper connection to one another existed.

Something crashed into the landfill, the sound coming from the northwest corner. They listened alertly.

"An animal, maybe? Squirrel?" Miranda offered when the movement from beyond ceased for a moment.

"That thing is bigger than a squirrel," Father Daniel surmised.

The reassuring news was that the howling had stopped a little while ago. If it had been a coyote that fell into the pit, it must've strayed from the pack.

A growl sounded from the darkness, followed by trash wrestling as the creature tried to regain its balance.

"That's a beast," Father Daniel said. He continued with a Bible passage, Revelation 11:7: "When they have finished their testimony, the beast that comes up out of the abyss will make war with them, and overcome them, and kill them."

THE HOLE

The Carlyle Dump opened in September 1970 and was met with much disdain by the community of Shady Springs. Although it passed every landfill requirement and regulation, the thought of decomposing waste frightened people. The location of the dump was hidden deep within the woodlands and sat a half-mile from any major road. The size of the initial design was roughly that of a football field: fifty-four yards by one hundred yards. Over the years, it decreased in scale and, as other landfill locations became available, the Carlyle Dump was used less and became neglected, which led to water contamination and the closure in 2000.

The concept for trash landfills is simple: dig a big hole, line it with hard clay or plastic to prevent wastewater from escaping into the ground, compact and cover the trash with soil daily, and repeat. Aiding in the prevention of contamination is a leachate collection system. Leachate is water that gets polluted by waste contact. It oozes to the bottom of a landfill and is collected by a system of pipes. The pumped leachate is treated at a wastewater treatment plant, and the solids removed from the leachate during this step are returned to the landfill or are sent to some other landfill. If leachate collection pipes clog up, and leachate remains in the landfill, fluids can build, and the resulting liquid pressure becomes the main force driving waste out of the bottom of the landfill when the bottom liner fails. This happened at Carlyle.

After discovery of the contamination, the pipes were repaired, and the remaining layer of trash was buried by twenty-four inches of earthen material per landfill closing procedure. Also, the typical procedure is to monitor it for years to ensure contamination no longer exists or develops again. This was done for the ten years following closure, and the area was deemed clean. The property, roughly 150 acres, was mostly woods except for the open area of the old landfill in the center. The hole remained deep, which gave the new owner of the property a bad idea: continue to use it as a dump illegally. This is called "open dumping" and is common throughout Illinois.

Open dumps pose a good deal of health, safety, and environmental threats: fire and explosions, inhalation of toxic gases, diseases carried by mosquitos, flies, and rodents, and contamination to drinking water, lakes, streams, and plant and wildlife habitats. To sum it up, the new owner of the Carlyle property was a stupid, stupid man.

Sixty-year-old Hubert Wilson was left a large inheritance from his father, which he used to purchase the inexpensive land, thinking he could then resell individual plots and become a millionaire. His stupidity kept him from understanding that no one wanted property on the site of an old, contaminated landfill. When his even dumber brother-in-law suggested reopening the landfill and operating it like a black-market dump, he saw dollar bills and jumped at the chance, since the rest of his inheritance had paid for a little cottage for him and his mother on the property. An injury at his old job prevented him from working, and he received disability checks that barely paid for his utilities. He wasn't a man of principles or integrity. He'd take a buck for an old, soiled pair of Fruit-of-the-Looms if offered.

When Carlyle closed, and the place was abandoned, an old, broken-down bulldozer was left behind. Hubert had a background in automobile mechanics, and with the help of the brother-in-law, he brought the old

Caterpillar back to life. He deepened the hole and got in and out of it via a narrow ramp that he later filled in— yet another ignorant act. He never thought he'd need to go back down there; his plan was to fill the hole to the surface and then to cover it with dirt. Had he done his research, he would've known he was brewing a toxic soup that only the devil could enjoy.

And the devil was alive and well.

THE BEAST

"Can someone please help me?" Colin asked, trying to move Punam. The group started retreating away from the beast in the darkness, and they didn't give a thought to helping Punam.

"Look, we can't save her. She's almost dead anyway. We need to think of ourselves right now," Glen said, his earlier concern a distant memory.

"You're a dick." Colin couldn't bite his tongue. What was the point of holding back in the current environment? Miranda stepped forward and grabbed Punam's other arm, and they raised her, the rustling trash approaching. They moved through the debris, each of them falling along the way to the other corner of the dump.

"Wait!" Father Daniel halted them. "Listen." They heard nothing following them.

"Why are we running? Look, I'll go back and check it out. Running through this shit isn't going to save us, anyway. We're gonna hit a fucking wall." Byron made his way back to base camp, armed with a piece of a two-by-four. When he arrived at the clearing, he scanned the perimeter, hoping to see a shadowy movement.

It jumped him from behind.

He fell to the ground, his weapon flying into the darkness. When he tried to get back up, he was attacked in the face—by wet, sloppy kisses from a large German shepherd.

"Holy shit!" Byron gasped as he pushed the dog off. "You almost died, dog." He stood and yelled to the cowering group in the corner, "It's only a dog!" He then muttered under his breath, "Fucking beast, my ass."

Helen was the first one back, excited to be in the company of a canine. It was a male dog, as Byron discovered when his hand had brushed against his penis while shoving him away. He was excited to see a little girl, and he proved it by greeting her with kisses. This brought Helen a slight sense of joy as she recalled her own dog, a little beagle named Beetles that had been a gift from her "aunt and uncle" when she was five. Beetles had been her buddy until she learned the true identities of the gift bearers. This knowledge momentarily damaged their relationship. Helen punished the dog by neglecting her. She stopped cuddling and fussing over him until her intellectual grandparents realized her displaced anger. They helped her understand she was taking out her anger at her parents on Beetles. After she dealt with some of the anger, things went back to normal. She once again loved Beets.

But she hated the two cats.

Her grandparents' cats were complete idiots. They often hid under the sofa or coffee table and attacked her ankles as she passed by them. She pleaded with her grandparents to have them declawed, but they refused, saying it was inhumane.

"But it's okay for them to scratch me up all the time?" Helen was nine, and the cats had been around since the day she was born.

"Child, wear socks," her grandmother suggested.

"Bullshit!"

"Excuse me, young lady?"

"I hate socks! Why should I have to wear them because of those stupid cats?" She was digging a hole she might not escape from.

A bit of foreshadowing.

"Go to your room. Now!" her grandmother ordered.

Her grandfather was out playing poker, and she dreaded these evenings because they always turned into heart-to-hearts with her grandma. Helen didn't want to talk about mushy stuff, and now she knew the way to avoid them: cursing.

She walked down to her bedroom in the basement of the fifties ranch home and plopped on her bed. The tiger cat that just scratched her followed her down. Her anger still at its height, she decided to punish the pussy. She pulled her pillow out of the pillowcase and chased the cat until she could scoop it up in the case. She swung the pillowcase full of cat all around the room, circle after circle, the cat initially crying but unable to catch its breath after a minute. And then she accidentally swung it into the metal support pole in the middle of her room. She heard the knock of bone to metal, which created a slight reverberation. She freaked and dropped the pillowcase; the cat fell out, lifeless. She held her hand to her mouth and muffled a cry. After a minute of anxiety, she bent down and studied the cat, its tongue hanging out of its mouth. It didn't take a genius to know it was dead. She stared at it for a long time, thinking it would come back to life. Cats had nine lives, didn't they?

And then she heard her grandmother descending the basement stairs.

Panicked, she shoved the cat back into the pillowcase and scanned the room for a hiding place, but there was no time. She threw it at the head of her bed and lay down, placing her head on the dead-cat pillow.

Grandma sat at the foot of the bed. "I'm sorry I yelled, sweetie."

"It's okay," Helen said and really meant it. The least she could do right now was mean it.

"You need to understand how very important my feline friends are to me and your grandfather. They are like our children, just like you. You all have different mommies and daddies, biologically speaking, but psychologically and emotionally, you are our children."

Helen forced a smile and adjusted her head atop one of her grandmother's dead children. Next came the story of how they'd gained Flimsy, and her guilt almost made her confess the accident.

Almost.

When Grams kissed her good night and settled onto the recliner upstairs, Helen sneaked out the basement door and flung Flimsy over the privacy fence, intending to land her in the neighbor's yard, but the fling was so powerful that she landed on the neighbor's roof.

It was days before the body was discovered. A heavy rainstorm washed it down and into the paper grocery bag of Mrs. Smittle, as she was unloading her car. It was the perfect basket and proof that it really could rain cats and dogs. Upon removal of the frozen chicken and Flimsy from the bag, many questions arose. Helen was interrogated at the kitchen table, pendant light directly above her like in the cop shows, and she lied through it but still ended up seeing a shrink, which turned out to be a blessing for her. She confessed the incident and got it off her chest.

Back in the darkness of the landfill, Helen suggested they name the dog after her beagle. "Let's name her Beets."

"That's a stupid name. Who the hell eats beets, anyway? Besides, it's he, not she," Byron said.

"Okay. Bee … Bees … How about Beef?"

"That's a terrible name, girl, but we may very well end up eating him, so Beef makes sense," Byron half-joked as Helen gave him the bird, aware he probably couldn't see it. The others made it back finally, and Punam was placed on the ground once again.

"Look, people, we need to arm ourselves. I say we all look for weapons," the sensible convict suggested. This seemed to upset Beef, as he started barking hysterically, seemingly at nothing. "Dude, shut the fuck up!"

"I sense a presence. Something else is in here with us," Father Daniel said.

"Yeah, sure. Just like you said this dog was a beast from hell." Byron felt around for another long, sharp piece of wood just outside the camp area. The dog continued to bark.

"It's okay, Beef. We're here, boy." Helen took ownership as the clouds rolled back in, covering the sky once more and stealing the light of the moon. They all readjusted their vision as downpour number two began.

"Fuck!" Byron yelled as Beef continued to bark and the others scrambled to rebuild their sorry shelter.

Anything pulled from the heaping piles was covered in stench and slime. The rain aided in cleansing, but it also created leachate. The toxic water traveled through the soiled ground and into the collection system, which had recently cracked again. It would soon be discovered that a nearby stream had been contaminated.

Beef sprung from Helen's side and ventured into the gorge. He was determined to uncover something. Rat? Snake?

"God, what is happening?" Mia screamed into the sky, her recent silence concluding. "Why would someone do this? Who could be so evil?" She cried.

Father Daniel, sensing she was attractive and knowing she was an actress, decided to help. "Let me comfort you, child. Come to me."

Mia felt her way to him as he once again held a flimsy sheet of cardboard over his head. She sat next to him, and he pushed her head into his chest as she continued to cry. Colin propped Punam so her face wasn't on the wet ground and wrapped another piece of material around her.

A flash of lightning surprised everyone, and the crack of thunder that followed provoked gasps from a couple of them.

They all settled back in their circle, creating a shelter that didn't keep the rain completely off them but prevented them from being soaked to the bone. Beef was still barking out in the rubble, and subsequent flashes of lightning lit his form. Three flashes of light later, Miranda screamed bloody murder.

"Did anyone else see that?"

"What?"

"That thing!" Beef's barking was more intense, as if he'd seen the thing as well. It was pitch black once again. "It was huge!"

"Probably a shadow," Glen suggested. Another flash. "Shit! I just saw it too."

Byron stood and looked toward the barking. He waited for the next flash. It wasn't coming, but he wanted an immediate answer. He wandered out with his wooden weapon, the bark about forty feet away. All senses were dulled. The patter of the rain, the barking, the thunder, the blackness, the rain in his eyes—all amounted to complete disorientation. Alcohol was not needed to achieve an effect of highness.

And then a monstrous wailing filled the air. An ear-piercing scream from something that wasn't human. Every hair on Byron's body stood at attention. It was a strange time to think of his former friend, Vincent, but he knew Vinnie would be intrigued by this situation. He used to insist Byron watch the horror classics with him, and this wailing reminded him of *An American Werewolf in London,* a film they had watched a handful of times together. The two Americans in the film were warned not to wander off the beaten path, but the dumbasses did anyway. It kind of served them right— the badness that followed. Byron wondered if he was being served right in this situation for wandering off the straight-and-narrow path of goodness.

Lightning flashed again, the strings of rain shining in front of him. When the light vanished, another wail filled the air very close to Byron. Almost on top of Byron.

The next flash of light revealed the furry monster staring directly into his eyes.

Miranda screamed.

The light and Byron disappeared.

THE TIRES

The rain ended close to sunset, and the group was swimming and dripping in toxic water. The little clearing called base camp was now polluted, the rain mixing everything in the landfill like a stew of death. The daylight and mounting sun sparked a necessary energy, and the hope of escape permeated the air and pierced through the odor.

The first order of business was finding Byron.

"He must have fallen and knocked himself out," Glen surmised, unwilling to believe he and Miranda had seen anything but a shadow. The tale of a beast grabbing Byron and taking him away was craziness.

Miranda fiercely disagreed. The beastly image had triggered a memory of a childhood trauma. At age ten, her father disappeared. He left for work one morning and never returned. She was convinced the monster under her bed had ripped Daddy apart limb from limb while she was at school. He had always thought her crazy and dragged her to the floor to prove there was no monster, but she couldn't be convinced. This monster could disappear at the snap of a finger, so of course he'd be gone when Daddy looked for him.

"He is visiting Grandma in Florida," Miranda's mother explained. This caused confusion: her father hated her grandma. He used words like bitch, asshole, and whore to describe her. Plus, he surely would've said goodbye or called Miranda. It had been two weeks and nothing from him.

And then the blood in the bed.

Miranda awoke from the nightmare of her father being mutilated by this beast only to find blood on her sheets. She screamed for her mother and cried that her suspicions were true: her father was dead under the bed, and the blood had soaked up through the sheets. Her mother joined in the sobbing, saddened that her little girl had become a woman and that she would now have to tell Miranda her hero father was a coward who'd abandoned the family. It took many years for Miranda to believe her father had left voluntarily. It was easier to believe the monster was responsible.

◎   ◎   ◎

"I know what I saw, Mr. Weatherman." Miranda wasn't imagining this disappearance or making false assumptions. She'd witnessed a large, ape-like creature grab Byron and disappear into the darkness.

"So, you're saying Bigfoot lives in this shithole? Where did he come from? How did he get down here? How did he get Byron out of here?"

"I don't fucking know that! All I know is what I saw."

"Nobody else saw that. Listen, it's okay. We're all a little stressed out here, hungry, disoriented, confused, and horny. We're going to hallucinate."

"Who the hell is horny? How can you think of sex in this filth? You're disgusting!" Miranda walked in the direction of the sighting as the others stared at Glen.

"I'm sorry, but this has to be the longest I've gone without sex. Sue me for being horny." Glen splashed through the wetness as he left camp. "Let's get out of here."

Father Daniel bit his tongue. Having Mia pressed against him throughout the night certainly aroused him as well. His nose also caught a hint of perfume, remarkable considering the odors and how filthy she must be.

"Wait!" Colin yelled as the group dispersed. "We need a plan. We can't just climb up a fifty-foot dirt wall. And by dirt, I mean mud."

They eyeballed the area, searching for a glaringly obvious plan for scaling the wall.

"Tires!" Glen shouted from afar. "There are tires everywhere down here. Let's stack them. Make a ladder with them."

And the tire hunt began. They drudged through the muck, which had risen a few inches from the rain; certain areas were knee deep. It was possible to sink below and never be found; half a football field was a large range. Glen's theory on Byron's whereabouts was not crazy. Miranda wasn't convinced. She wasn't looking for tires; she was searching for Byron, determined to prove Glen wrong. She never really liked the guy she saw on her television. He always seemed dramatic and pretentious as he discussed weather patterns and windstorms. And the stories at the nail salon from multiple female sources indicated he was a womanizing prick.

Beef followed Miranda and sniffed the area as she tossed things aside, searching for the missing man.

"Can you stay with her, please?" Colin asked Father Daniel, grabbing his hand, and directing him to Punam, who was once again propped up and mostly out of the waste. Colin was amazed she was still breathing. She had to be fighting something deep within, and it was a bout she was winning. For now.

"What do I do?"

"Just keep her propped up against this skid."

"What if she starts screaming and calling me names?"

"Hug her hard. Pray for her, Father. That is what you do, right? You have faith, don't you?"

Daniel smiled and nodded. He liked to think a little faith existed, but again, nothing significant solidified that thought. But perhaps this moment, not just caring for Punam, but this larger moment of captivity with the imminent threat of death would spark faith. This could be his time to shine, to take the lead acting role. He needed to come up with a title for this production. Which genre would it fall under? His newfound purpose in the hole excited him as he slid next to Punam and hugged her. And then his savior thoughts screeched to a halt when his arm brushed against her perky breasts. He couldn't control the sexual thoughts, for he hadn't been so close to multiple women in decades, since before his role of priest.

Glen attempted the tire stacking, having three within his reach, but he lacked a solid foundation. It seemed the deepest parts of the rubbish were against the walls, and the weight of the tires caused shifts in the trash, eliminating stability. He needed to clear an area before recovering any more tires.

Helen joined Miranda and Beef in the search for the convict.

"Are you sure you didn't see anything last night?" Miranda asked Helen. She believed other people had spotted the creature but doubted their vision. It was possible someone was holding back for fear of being labeled as crazy, like Miranda. At least the wailing of the beast couldn't be denied, could it?

"No. But my grandma always told me there is no such thing as monsters. That monsters are only your insecure mind fighting for clarity."

"Huh? What the hell kind of bullshit is that? Your grandma sounds like a psycho." Miranda chuckled.

Helen laughed. "I'm not even sure what that means. She said it so many times, I just sort of remember it." It seemed they both had monsters under their beds. "Do you have kids?"

Miranda's smile faded. "I have three boys." She fretted that she should be thinking more about her children right now instead of herself. What was happening to them in her absence? "They must be worried out of their minds. My hope is Bucky, my eleven-year-old, steps up to the plate to look after his younger brothers. But he can be a stubborn little bastard, so all bets are off."

"Why are we here? And where are we, anyway? Shady Springs?"

"I don't know the answers, honey. Look up—there is nothing but trees and the sky. It looks like that in Shady Springs and Timbuk-fucking-tu. There's nothing to give us any clue where we are. The why? Who knows? There are sick, crazy people out there who love to torment other people. I saw in the news the other day—and I can't tell you what day it was—that some girl was kidnapped, and parts of her body were cut off and sent to her parents until they paid a ransom. They got her back, minus some fingers and toes, but never found the guy. People disappear off the face of the earth every day, never to be found. Maybe they all end up in a hole like this one." She looked down at Helen and realized she might be scaring the girl. "I'm sorry, honey. I didn't mean us. We're getting the hell out of here."

"With all our fingers?"

"Yes."

"But the monster?"

"Maybe it was all my imagination. I'm sure it was, honey," she fibbed as they kicked around in the four-foot deep stew, Beef's head barely above the surface. They turned up nothing. "Okay, let's go help with the tires." They left the location of Byron's disappearance as Miranda's thoughts shifted from the beast to her children and Bucky tormenting his brothers in her absence.

Glen discovered the northwest corner of the landfill was mostly clear with shallow rainwater, and he called for the others to bring their treasures of tires over to him. This task was extremely time-consuming, as the walk was lengthy from one side to the other and the navigation through the waste was treacherous because pieces of wood or trash under the surface contained sharp points. The threat of being impaled was real. Once the stack was five tires high, they started slipping away from each other, the thick coatings of slime wreaking havoc on stability. Halfway through the day, the blistering sun and no water or nourishment took their toll on the group. Many of them had to rest, and the sightings of tires became scarce. They needed roughly sixty tires—if they were ten inches in thickness—to scale the fifty-foot wall. They currently counted thirty.

A while later, they counted ten tires and eight feet high. A new achievement without collapsing. Glen was proud of the progress. He instructed everyone to support the base of the tire stack while the smallest person, Helen, climbed to the top.

"That's not high enough. Shouldn't we continue to stack?" Mia asked, frustrated the task was taking so long, as nightfall was just around the corner.

"It's a test. It will only take a minute."

The group surrounded the tire stack, and Glen motioned for Helen to begin. The tires were various sizes, which allowed little stepping gaps, best suited for small feet. Helen placed her dirty, wet, right sneaker on the bottom step and grabbed a tire above her as a handle. She worked her way up three tires and then hit an extremely slimy one and slipped, falling onto Glen's head, dragging the top four tires down with her.

"This is a waste of time! This will never work!" Mia screamed.

"You have any other ideas, lady?"

"I'm Mia. My name is Mia!"

"Mamma Mia! C'mon, stack them back up. Look for sharp sticks or anything that can pierce this rubber. We'll have to stitch them together, keep them from sliding apart."

They separated, following leader Glen's instructions. Hope was fading like the sun above. If they couldn't get ten tires to stay together, how could they get thirty? Or sixty? And they were all hungry now. The pains were getting worse.

"Do we have a plan for food?" Colin asked, everyone still within earshot.

"Food plan? Yeah. We get out of here and grab a burger," Glen said. "There's nothing to eat down here."

"A fucking burger. That sounds amazing," Miranda muttered next to Helen, the only one hearing and smiling.

Helen closed her eyes. "A burger with cheese and fried onions."

"Really? You like fried onions? Those things give me heartburn. But you're young. You can handle it." Miranda patted Helen's back, which was wet from the tire fall.

"We're not getting out of here today, are we?"

"We are certainly going to try, dear."

"Yeah, but we're not getting out of here today. A lot of day is gone, and we're not even close."

Helen spoke the truth, and Miranda couldn't deny it, but she chose to focus on finding materials to spike those stupid rubber slime tubes together. She fought to keep her mind off the beast and the fear of it returning if they were stuck down here for another night. It was alarming how quickly Byron was forgotten. His name hadn't been mentioned again since the morning. With all the tire excavations, he would've turned up; she was sure of it. Glen's conclusion was wrong.

The sun helped to dry some toxic water puddles, and then it disappeared behind a tree, losing yellow and warmth, which triggered a hustle from the exhausted group. The ten-step tire ladder was slowly sutured and stabilized. Helen was summoned for attempt number two. After nearly slipping on the third step, she successfully made it to the top and stood, each foot on a side of the top tire: King of the Hill in the hellhole. A tongue twister for the suffering victims.

Colin had checked out of the tire-ladder project an hour earlier, determined to revamp the center base camp, knowing they weren't leaving. He cleared debris and lined the ground with spare tires: this would keep them out of the contaminated mud and prevent them from swimming if the rain returned. He then speared corners of the tires, creating a roof support. The search for roof material was next, and while he searched for flat material, he grabbed a bloated trash bag or two and gave them to Father Daniel to inspect for anything edible. Punam was next to him on her side, her breathing shallow.

Beef barked at Helen, who was still perched atop the tires, unable to get down for fear she would slip and fall onto something sharp. She wasn't in the mood for an impaling. She thought of her grandfather lecturing her on safety, of how he and Grandma would be devastated if anything ever happened to her. She suddenly longed for a hug and hoped they weren't thinking the worst had happened to their adopted daughter.

"Sit on the edge and jump. I'll catch you," Glen suggested, on the verge of losing his cool as he realized his wonderful escape plan was full of flat tires. He was not sure how they would continue to stack them. They couldn't hand them up gracefully, so throwing them was their only option, and the girl didn't have the strength to catch the larger truck tires.

Helen carefully sat on the edge of the top tire and dangled her feet down toward Glen, but before he reached for them, she slipped and fell backward into the tire hole. She screamed as she softly landed on her head, her arms and legs spreading on the way down, catching onto tire lips to cushion her fall. She had finally achieved a headstand—something that had eluded her in gym class. She peered into the inner black rubber tube of the bottom tire and caught a movement. A fuzzy leg poked out. Then another, and another, and then the two beady little eyes of a tarantula-like spider made their appearance. Helen screamed and tried to move, but she was wedged like a cork in a wine bottle.

The spider was five inches from her face and moving in for a closer look.

THE BEEF

“Are you okay?” Miranda yelled into the tire tube as Beef increased his barking, wondering the same. As Glen attempted to climb the tires, Beef grabbed his pant leg and pulled him back.

"I'm trying to help her, dumbass!" Glen tried to kick the German shepherd, but the dog jumped to the side, narrowly missing the flying foot.

"What are you doing? Don't touch the dog," Miranda said. "Are you okay, Helen?"

Helen couldn't answer. She was too busy spitting and blowing at the approaching eight-legged freak. "Fine, fuck it. I can't help with this fucking dog trying to eat me." Glen walked away from the scene toward the renovated base camp.

Miranda and Mia shook their heads in disgust and started ripping the tires from their sewn positions, destroying the work that had taken all day. Glen turned back and caught the action but did not stop them. Defeat clouded the air, fighting the stench of rot.

Beef calmed as he watched the ladies. He was trained to help those in need, but he knew his limitations. For the moment, he relished his freedom, even if it was within the confines of the landfill. It was only hours ago he'd been locked in a cage.

◎　　◎　　◎

Beef was part of an eight-puppy litter that had been bred and sold to the Chicago Police Department seven years earlier. He was the standout of the litter, excelling faster than the others in obedience training and detection, and search and rescue training. His sense of smell pierced through paper- and plastic-coated vessels of cocaine and marijuana. He could even smell it inside a person—through skin and muscle. Even feces from a drug mule didn't hide the smell.

"C'mere, Chad," Officer Greenwell said, motioning for the dog now called Beef. Beef was formerly named after a fallen officer, which was standard procedure. This was how all the K9s were named—a way of honoring those lost in the line of duty. "Guess what, my friend? It's time to work." Bruce Greenwell had just been called for backup at a house suspected of hiding a meth lab in the basement. If meth was produced there, Chad could tell them before the raid.

At three years of age, Beef had assisted in over fifty drug-possession arrests and had helped locate twenty missing persons, both alive and deceased. As was customary, he lived with an officer and came to work as needed. He enjoyed the company of the police department, especially when he didn't have to go out in the treacherous fields of Chicago. Fetch and neck rubs were more enjoyable than potential death by gunfire, but he was always up for challenges.

"Wanna go to Oz later?" Officer Greenwell asked Chad as he drove them to the south side and the location of their assignment.

Chad excitedly paced in the back seat. Oz was a park and a buzzword. This was a park in Chicago dedicated to the author of *The Wonderful Wizard of Oz*, L. Frank Baum, who settled in the big city in 1891 several miles west of the park. Greenwell was a six-foot-tall tough man on the field but a gentle giant when in Oz, reliving childhood viewing memories of the classic film as he and Chad passed the monuments of Tin Man and Scarecrow.

They arrived a block away from the targeted house and parked out of sight. Greenwell and Chad approached four other officers and received the intel. Neighbors had been calling the PD for the last week, claiming strong odors were coming from the dilapidated house and suspicious activities were happening - weird-looking visitors at all hours of the night and strange-smelling backyard fires. This was probable suspicion of a meth lab. Chad's sniff of approval was the icing missing from the double-layered meth cake.

As Greenwell and K9 strolled the perimeter of the house, Chad did not indicate that meth or any type of drug was inside. Perhaps this meth cake was icing less?

"Are you sure, boy?"

Chad sat and stared at his owner after the walk-and-sniff. Greenwell pulled a treat from his pocket, and Chad gingerly took it from his hand.

"Let's try again."

They repeated the perimeter sweep. Chad smelled the doorways and the glass-blocked basement windows. After lap two, Chad sat and gave his partner the same look.

"But the windows are all blackened," one of the four other officers noted as Greenwell shared the news around the corner from the house. Windows with trash bags or newspapers taped to them was an obvious sign something was happening inside the inhabitants didn't want the world to see.

Greenwell's walkie beeped.

The head of the narcotics department was calling, prepared to move a crew out to the house to immediately diffuse and clean any type of meth lab. Greenwell broke the news of the paws-down from Chad. They were given the orders to move out. As they were packing up, they heard a scream coming from the direction of the house. Greenwell motioned for two of the other officers to follow him. Chad brought up the rear.

As they rounded a tall set of bushes, the two-story house was once again in view. A woman was struggling to open the upstairs window, but it wouldn't go higher than eight inches. She put her mouth to the opening and screamed once again.

"Please, help me!"

Greenwell motioned for her to keep quiet as he and the other officers hurried to the side door. In a three count, they kicked the door open. Chad ran in ahead of them in his search-and-rescue mode. Guns drawn, the three officers covered one another as they moved about the darkened house, flashlights blazing, their eyes peeled for potential human threats and evidence of meth production as they made it to the stairs. Chad started barking upstairs, already at the victim's door.

"Is she in there, boy?" Chad barked again as the three officers approached. The door was padlocked from the outside. "Miss, are you alright?" Greenwell asked.

"No, I'm bleeding. Please get me out!"

"Who did this to you? Do you know if anyone else is here?"

"In the basement. Please get me out of here."

"How many?"

"Three, I think. There are three coffins."

Alarmed, the officers looked at each other. "You stay and get her out. We'll go to the basement with Chad," Officer Jeng ordered. "And call for backup. We'll call the other officers back as well." They called for help and split up, leaving Greenwell alone outside the padlocked bedroom door.

"Stand back, miss." He lifted his right foot and kicked into the door, pushing it open an inch, but it was still attached by the padlock. The woman poked her bloody fingers through the crack. "Please, miss, stand back. I'm kicking again." Her fingers vanished as he rushed the door with his large frame, ramming it and separating the door from the lock. It flew open, crashing into the wall behind.

"Thank you!"

He shined the light into the woman's face. She looked pale and sick, blood running from her neck. "How long have you been here?"

"I don't know. Days?"

"What'd they do to you?" Greenwell asked as she approached him, crying. "Please, Miss, do not come any further. Please stay where you are." He shined his flashlight around the darkened room, which was void of furniture except for a filthy twin mattress in the corner. His light also caught a set of metal dog bowls, one with water, the other with remnants of possibly food stuck to the sides. It seemed this woman had been shackled like an outside dog, a chain wrapped around her leg, the other end screwed to the wall. He lowered his gun, and she rushed him, wrapping her arms around him and sobbing into his neck. "It's okay. It's going to be alright. What's your name, Miss?"

"I haven't eaten in days." She opened her mouth, plunged her razor-sharp fangs into his neck, and ripped a huge chunk of flesh from his body, sending a thick spray of blood all over the room as he dropped his flashlight and gun and fell to the ground. He struggled for a moment, but the blood loss quickly zapped his energy.

Chad was the only one to hear the faint cry from his buddy upstairs and immediately left the other officers. When he got back to the room, he saw the woman eating a chunk of his beloved best friend. He went to Greenwell and sniffed, discovering he was deceased. He let out an ear-piercing howl of despair and attacked the woman, ripping off her ear and giving her a taste of her own brutality. He then ripped her throat open, and she fell atop and died on Greenwell.

Chad lay next to Greenwell and put his head on his chest. He didn't move until he was forced to move after the mutilation was discovered a short while later. The deceased woman had been brainwashed into believing she'd been turned into a vampire and all she could eat was flesh and blood. Several people were murdered in the house, their blood removed and bodies burned out back, the smell alerting the neighbors. Three residents of the house were discovered in the basement in poorly made coffins, also believing they were blood-sucking monsters.

The K9 was fired from the police department and was to be euthanized for the murder of the woman. While the officers understood his motive, it couldn't go unpunished. He was trained to protect and serve, never to kill.

Officer Jeng was assigned the transfer of Chad to the veterinary hospital of death, but he had second thoughts on the way. He decided to spare Chad, driving him slightly outside of Chicago to Shady Springs and releasing him into a wooded area.

"Bruce loved you, boy. He did. Never forget. He'll always be right here." Jeng patted Chad's underside and hugged him. "You can start a new life here. Peace and love to you, my friend."

Jeng jumped back into the car and raced away. Chad chased the car for half a mile and stopped at a gravel driveway. He followed it up a hill until he came upon a little cottage.

"What the fuck do you want? Where'd you come from?" a gray-haired man asked as he closed the front door of the cottage.

Chad realized he was in trouble, but he was so exhausted from the run and the mental stress of the last few days that he didn't fight when the old man grabbed him by the scruff of his neck and threw him into the toolshed. He remained a captive in the dirty, dark shed for five days with no food or water while Hubert built a cage outside. When the door finally opened, he walked outside to his new enclosed home and was greeted by another old human—a woman.

"Well, looky what we got here. Where'd you come from? You sher do stink, boy." The woman slid two metal bowls under the metal fencing, one for food and one for water. Chad ate and drank the bowls clean while the old woman watched. "Now, don't get too used to that. We ain't got money to feed you every day, ya hear? I tell you what. You let us know when you see vermin out here. We'll shoot the sons of bitches, and then you'll getta eat. How 'bout that? Think you can handle that, stinker? Now, what should we call ya?"

* * *

"Thank you," Helen said, finally upright and freed, the tire ladder demolished, and the nasty spider no longer terrorizing the girl. The former K9 licked her hand, and she knelt to hug him. "Thank you for trying to help me, Beef. You're the best dog ever."

Mia looked at the pile of tires, and Beef saw sadness in her face. This was not the solution to the problem. They would not escape by stacking tires.

The three turned and started for the center, each anxious about what was in store on their second night of darkness. As they neared the revamped base camp, they heard pops in the distance. Sounded like fireworks. Beef barked.

"Fuck!" Glen grabbed his arm. Blood began flowing down to his hand. He had been shot in the arm; the fireworks were gunfire from a figure standing above ground at the corner of the hole directly above the failed escape plan. "Take cover! We're being attacked!"

Everyone scurried to the inside of the shelter, hoping to hide themselves from the crazy person shooting at them.

"Pecker! Get back up here, you traitor!" Hubert shouted at the dog. "These assholes aren't your friends." He shot at Beef again and missed him but hit a branch holding up part of the shelter's roof. It collapsed, eliciting screams.

"Please stop! Why are you doing this?" Miranda yelled.

Hubert lowered his shotgun and disappeared, frustrated that his imprisoned dog he called *Pecker* had escaped.

THE AGENT

"What part of *'stop at the old Carlyle Dump'* did you not understand, Ryan?" Jamal asked.

This was Ryan's third month with Illinois Waste Control (IWC) and based on the tone of his supervisor he feared he wouldn't make it to a fourth month. Ryan's official title was Regulatory Compliance Analyst, which encompassed many duties and responsibilities, including testing for contamination in streams within proximity to closed landfills. This was his uncompleted task for the day. "I totally ran out of time. I sincerely apologize." This wasn't the first time Ryan had sincerely apologized for not completing a task.

"How is that possible? You only had a handful of appointments today." Jamal told Ryan he had been more than patient with the young man, and that having worked his way up the ranks at IWC for the last twenty years, he knew what it took to become successful. He also brutally concluded out loud to Ryan that he didn't have what it took. "Why didn't you work over a little?"

"I can't today, sir. I have an important personal activity this evening."

"If I would've asked you to work over today, you would have to. You know that, right?"

"Um, yeah, sure, sir."

Jamal gave Ryan a hard, intimidating stare, forcing him to look out the window and clear his throat, ending the awkward silence.

A white bird slammed into the window and flipped backward, flopping to the ground outside the first-floor office. Ryan exhaled the startle away and took a deep breath.

"Holy Christ!" Jamal said as they both walked to the window and laid eyes on the bird with a broken neck, dead in the grass. "Poor bastard."

"This is not good, sir."

"I know it's sad, Ryan, but a dead bird is minor to what's happening in the world today."

"No, I mean, this means something bad will happen. Death. It's an omen."

Jamal pointed to the bird. "Yes, Ryan, death did happen."

"No. To me or you. It's a warning. Now I'm concerned. Maybe I shouldn't propose to Rebecca tonight."

"Oh, wow, that's your personal business? Why didn't you tell me? Congrats!" Jamal patted Ryan on the back. Perhaps this proposal story would save his job.

"Don't congratulate me. This may be a sign not to marry Rebecca. She could bring me years of unhappiness until I die in a freak waterskiing accident."

"What? You're a fool."

"No, sir. The writing is on the glass." Ryan pointed to a line of blood on the window starting at the point of bird contact. "I wonder where the blood came from. Its beak, maybe?"

"Alright, look now, I demand you leave here at once and get yourself engaged. You can stop at the Carlyle Dump first thing in the morning."

"I will definitely continue in the morning, but it might not be as an engaged man."

Ryan grabbed his messenger bag and quickly exited Jamal's office. On his way to his car, he thought hard about his decision to marry Rebecca.

Rebecca had been Ryan's high school sweetheart. This was a love that survived college and Ryan's periodic desires to have sex with others. She was the only girl he'd ever had sex with, which led him to question his commitment, but he genuinely loved her and wanted to spend the rest of his life with her. So, he buried the need to gather *strange*, as the cool dudes called it. Ryan was never cool, though. He was classified as nerdy and eccentric. He was highly intelligent but lacked focus. His parents were encouraged by high school faculty to have him tested for attention deficit hyperactivity disorder, famously known as ADHD. They refused to believe it was anything chemical. They decided he needed more discipline, so they forced him to excel. He had no life in high school because he was constantly grounded or locked in his bedroom and forced to study. Rebecca was his only source of pleasure and familial escape.

Ryan's focus in college was controlled by Rebecca as well. They both attended Chicago State University and lived with Rebecca's aunt, which proved a complicated living arrangement.

"She's right under us," Rebecca reminded Ryan as he slid his hand down her V-neck T-shirt and groped her left breast. It was three months into freshman year, and they had yet to christen their college experience.

"So, we aren't ever having sex again? Is that what I'm to understand?" Ryan was frustrated. If he could jerk off twice a day in the house with Aunt Marjorie in the next room, why couldn't they discreetly have sex?

"We need to wait for her to leave the house."

"She never leaves the house! Why does she never leave the house? Is she agoraphobic?"

"She does leave the house. It's just that we're at class when she does."

"Oh, I understand. Okay, well, if you'll excuse me, I'm going to whack my pud."

Ryan left their room and crossed the hall to the bathroom. Rebecca rolled her eyes and continued to study. Knowing masturbating helped him focus; she was fine with it.

"Do you want a foot-long wiener for dinner?" Aunt Marjorie called upstairs.

"No. No, she doesn't!" Ryan yelled from the bathroom.

They did have foot-longs for dinner that evening, and two weeks later, Rebecca had half a foot-long, as her aunt finally left the house.

◉　◉　◉

Ryan was on his way home to the tiny apartment he and Rebecca rented after college graduation in a suburb of Chicago. He had the engagement ring in his lap, which he had pulled from the glove box. It had lived there for three months as Ryan debated the proper presentation moment. At least that was what he thought the holdup was, but now it seemed he might not want to be married to Rebecca. The dead bird illuminated another perspective. He didn't want to believe his life was literally in danger if he married Rebecca, but there was a big, wide world he hadn't experienced yet, and marriage would kill his independence. The death of independence: that's what the bloody bird warned.

He decided to look for more clues when he got home to help determine his next move in the chess game of life.

"Honey, I'm home."

He closed the apartment door behind him and walked through the short entranceway, looking at the photos of him and Rebecca. A trip to New York. Horseback riding in Ohio. Screaming on a roller coaster at Six Flags. He really looked at these framed memories, unlike typical days of walking past them and ignoring them. Rebecca brought a smile to his face in every one of the photos. He imagined her smile-less face after telling her he didn't want to marry. But this was his own mind creating the scenario. She did not know he was even contemplating it. They rarely ever discussed it. So why was he obsessing over marriage? Today was their six-year anniversary, and if a proposal was to happen, it should be on a special day.

"Hi." Rebecca appeared and startled him.

She looked beautiful. Her shoulder-length auburn hair caught a ray of light from the descending sun in the window behind her. Her fair complexion allowed the freckles to fight for attention, and the one above her upper lip seemed to win the battle. He kissed her, as was the normal event after a day on the job. This kiss was different, though, as all senses were on high alert. He felt her lips with his lips. It was comforting, like that favorite food you long for when you're not feeling well.

"You look really pretty," he told her.

She laughed. "Really? You do see this T-shirt I have on, right? You know, I looked much better yesterday." Rebecca was never good at taking compliments. It was something she said rarely happened in her family during childhood. She plopped down on the sofa. "You want to just order a pizza tonight?" She grabbed an issue of *Entertainment Weekly* from the coffee table and started skimming through. It became clear she either didn't remember it was their sixth anniversary, or she didn't care about it. The next move belonged to him in this chess game.

"Are you sure you don't want an entrée a little more special today?"

Rebecca peeked at Ryan above Emma Stone, trying to understand why he'd asked that question. It wasn't her birthday or his. "Did you get promoted?"

"Funny. I almost got fired."

"Today is a special day?" she asked, totally oblivious. And she was usually great with remembering special occasions.

Ryan then realized if he didn't present her with the ring, he would have nothing else to give her for their anniversary. He hadn't picked up flowers or chocolates or anything else. He suddenly felt a huge pressure to decide. Should he propose?

"Oh. Cramps." He quickly left the room and squeezed into the tiny bathroom, anxiety overcoming him, as well as IBS. While he took care of business Rebecca scanned her social media pages, looking for something indicating why the day was special. She found nothing but Pudding Appreciation Day. There was a day for everything it seemed.

Ryan finished his IBS Appreciation Day and flushed the toilet. A decision, based on signs, had been made. He was ready for the checkmate.

"I'm sorry, Ryan, I totally forgot." Rebecca was standing with her arms spread, a huge smile on her face. Ryan approached her, and she wrapped her arms around him. "I'll make it up to you tomorrow. I guess I didn't know pudding meant that much to you." She giggled.

"Huh? No!" He pulled the ring box out of his pocket and got down on his right knee. Rebecca's smile disappeared. "Today is our sixth anniversary, and I would very much like it to be our last as an unmarried couple. So, if you could do me the honor of being my wife, I—"

"Today is not our anniversary, Ryan. It's next month."

"Shit." Ryan stood, embarrassed. "Okay, oops. Um, do you still want to get married, or should I try this again next month?"

"I never said yes, Ryan. I figured we would talk about marriage before this ever happened. I'm sorry. I'm not ready for that. We're just starting our life together now. We're finally done with school and able to spend more quality time with each other, and I like that. I don't need a piece of paper."

"Okay."

"And I'm scared. I'm scared we're not going to last. I'm scared we're going to wonder what we've missed by only ever being with each other."

Ryan needed to pick his face up off the floor. Rebecca was saying the exact words he'd muttered to himself when he was alone. The same words that kept him awake at night.

"And I know you feel the same way because you've said it in your sleep, Ryan." So, apparently, he wasn't kept awake at night by these thoughts. He spoke of them in his sleep. Awkward. "That's why I'm confused about this proposal."

"It was the bird. The dead bird. The sign. My job problems."

"What on earth are you talking about? You're crazy talking right now. Look, I have spent most of our relationship being your nurse or your mother. I don't know if I can do it forever. I'm sorry."

Ryan couldn't figure everything out in his head. Were they ending? If so, wasn't this kind of what he wanted? Or did he just want a break? Too many scenarios open to interpretation.

"What do you want to do?" Ryan finally asked.

"Why don't I stay with Katie for a while until we figure things out?" She walked to the bedroom and came back out with a suitcase, already packed.

"You've been planning this?"

"Yes. What a coincidence it's all worked out the way it has."

Rebecca chuckled nervously as Ryan tried to make sense of everything. One minute she was saying how great it was that they could spend quality time with each other post college, and the next she was packed and ready to spend zero quality time with him. Somehow, he had prompted the truth from her. All because of the stupidly timed proposal.

"How long will you be gone?"

"Not sure. Let's play it by ear."

"Will you be seeing other guys? Are we seeing other people during this time away from one another?"

"Isn't that the point of it all? Isn't that what you wanted when you were moaning random girls' names in your sleep with a hard-on?"

"What?"

"Yes, Ryan. Who were these women?"

"I had a hard-on?" Ryan was intrigued—wet dreams were something he never thought he had. He even wrapped tape around his penis a few times before bed only to find it completely intact in the morning.

"Okay, I'm leaving. Let's touch base in a few days. Goodbye."

She kissed him on the cheek and walked to the door only to spin around and walk back to him. He thought it was for one more tearful goodbye, but she leaned next to him, grabbed the *Entertainment Weekly* with Emma Stone on the cover, and quickly exited the apartment.

Ryan fell back onto the sofa and replayed the events of the last few minutes, puzzled by how things had escalated so quickly. He felt a sense of sadness coupled with a sense of relief, the same relief he'd seen in Rebecca's face when she dragged her suitcase out of the bedroom. Had living with him all these years been that stressful and exhausting? Had they both been unhappy all these years, and if so, why hadn't they ever discussed things?

Ryan envisioned the dead white bird in the grass under the window, turning its broken neck toward him and squawking with uncontrollable laughter. And as Ryan sat there fretting over the correlation of the dead bird and his dead relationship, he did not know the real sign had yet to be seen.

THE SENATOR

Glen wrapped his right arm slightly above the elbow where the bullet had removed a chunk of flesh. He was in an intense amount of pain and had no problem sharing. His cries and gasps for air were weighing on his fellow sewer rats.

"Pressure will help with that." Colin showed Glen how to tighten the dirty shirt around his arm, which made him wince in agony. Mia put her hands to her ears.

"What? This fucking hurts, lady!"

"Mia. Again, my name is Mia." She shifted her body to look away from Glen. The group was sitting on tires under the roof Colin had repaired after the gunfire threatened to take it all down.

"Which one of you is working with that crazy man?" Miranda had asked after the man above disappeared. They stared blankly. "He specifically called someone a pecker. My guess is that it must be one of the men. Do any of you know this asshole?" The guys shook their heads. "Then what did he mean, Pecker?"

Beef barked at Miranda.

"Pecker?" Beef barked again. "Holy shit, I think we've found our Pecker."

"That's mean. He's the pecker," Helen said as she pointed to a spot where the gunman stood.

The group discussed Beef and the man and concluded that they must both live on the property of the landfill. This didn't explain any connection between him and the residents of his hole, though.

"Your name is Beef now, not Pecker. Look at me, no more Pecker!" Helen told the dog, expecting him to understand.

"That is something my mother used to tell me," Miranda said and chuckled, shaking her head. "I dated around a bit in high school but couldn't really settle on one guy. I wasn't boning them all. But that didn't matter. Kids still thought I was a whore."

"That's not fair," said Helen.

"At the beginning, no, it wasn't. But once I got the reputation, I said fuck it—" Miranda looked at the girl.

"Sorry, I meant screw it. And I did. I screwed a bunch of them."

"That's a great story to share with the kid," Glen said quietly, still trying to manage his pain.

Miranda shot him a murderous look and sat on her designated tire, her ass sliding off and hitting the ground in the center of the rubber donut.

The sun had gone completely, but light still shone in the sky. Probably another hour before the black returned. And they hadn't discussed any sort of backup escape plan; the gunfire had sidetracked their thoughts. Punam was still unconscious but breathing. Colin kept her wounds as clean as possible, which was nearly impossible, as nothing sanitary existed anywhere in the hole besides a couple articles of clothing he wrung out in the rain. The hunger pains were excruciating and Father Daniel's trash-bag searches for food literally came up fruitless. He dug through milk cartons, rotten produce, slimy food containers, and occasionally dirty diapers. They avoided the topic of food, not wanting to make the stomach pains worse.

Beef caught a scent and left Helen's side. He trekked to the east side of the trash graveyard. Most of the toxic wetness had filtered down into the leachate trenches under the ground, which made it easier for the canine to navigate. When he was ten feet away, he began barking aggressively at the wall of dirt.

"Dumb dog," Glen mumbled. "Pecker was a good name for him." He laughed at his comic wit and then grimaced at his arm pain.

"You deserved to be shot. You deserve to be down here." Helen stood and headed to the dog.

"Says the girl whose life I saved. Whatever."

"Wait!" Miranda slipped off Punam's right loafer and took it to Helen. "Here, you can't keep walking around shoeless."

Helen slipped on the shoe which was three inches too big and smelled like sauerkraut, which would seem disgusting on a normal, non-life-threatening day, but today it made her hungry for the pork hot dogs and kraut her grandmother used to make in the crock pot. She thanked Miranda, and the two of them made their way to Beef, who continued to bark.

"Can I do anything for anyone?" Colin scanned the fort he'd built. Father Daniel was still next to Punam. Mia was in a tire next to Colin. Glen was four tires away.

"Yes. Can you tell me why we're down here? Can you tell me why we deserve to rot to death? I mean, that is what's gonna happen, correct?" the priest asked, which slightly tarnished Colin's hope of survival.

"I'm confused." Colin stood and rammed his head into a piece of board acting as a roof. It fell to the ground, narrowly missing Mia. She gasped and stood, helping him refasten it to the beams. Colin frowned. "Shouldn't you be comforting us, Father? That is your job, right? Shouldn't you at least have a little hope? You're a Catholic priest, right?" Daniel nodded. "So, what about the light of God? Can you describe it? Have you experienced that light?"

"No, young man, I cannot talk about the light. How could I talk about the light when I can't see out of my eyes?"

"I'm talking metaphorical, not literal. Are you one of those sad-sacked, nonbelieving, boozing priests we see in movies?"

"Yes, son, as a matter of fact, I am. Sorry to disappoint you. But I can pray for us if you'd like. I can spit words out of my mouth as well as any of those priests you see in the movies. Would you like me to do that?"

Colin felt sucker punched. If the moments when he sought comfort in church services ended with a sermon such as the one Father Daniel just gave, he would've abandoned all hope of a higher power existing years ago. Colin sat and tried to control his emotions.

Mia bent over Colin and hugged him. "Come on, Father. You can't be serious here. Whether or not you believe, you are doing the work of the Lord. He is channeling something through you to your congregation. I'm sure they feel spiritual sincerity from you, otherwise they wouldn't attend your services."

Colin wiped his face. "Look, someone special to me could be fighting for his life right now, or he could be dead. I have no idea what is happening to him. I feel completely helpless. And the situation we're all in down here—I just don't know."

"Look, Colin, I apologize. I know religion isn't your thing, but if you'd like me to pray, I will. I do know every prayer out there, and I can make them sound great. I love to act after all."

"Not sure that's helping," Mia said. "And I'm the actor in this group. You keep your title of priest, and I'll be the actress." She stuck her tongue out at the blind, fake man of God, which brought a smile to Colin's face.

"This is one fucked-up group," Glen chimed in from his tire recliner. "Probably why we're down here. We're being punished."

"Speak for yourself. What did you do to deserve this?" Mia asked.

Before Glen could answer, Punam kicked her foot in the air and landed her big toe in Daniel's mouth, creating the torture technique kids called the *fishhook*. He gagged and grabbed her foot, ripping the toe out of his mouth. Her toenail scratched the roof of his mouth, producing blood that he immediately spat onto Colin.

"Hey!" Colin said.

"Son of a bitch! For someone on her deathbed, this lady has a lot of fight." Daniel crawled out of his tire and stumbled around the cleared area of the base camp.

Punam did not give up. She was trapped in her damaged body yet fueled with the need for answers. Was that her kidnapped daughter the old woman pulled out of the potato sack, and if so, was she dead?

Glen was glad the ruckus had occurred, so he didn't have to answer the question of what he'd done to deserve the punishment he was suffering.

Back at the wall of dirt, Helen and Miranda were calming Beef. His search and rescue training with the

Chicago PD had taught him to recognize the smell of decomposed humans, and Beef had discovered just that aroma coming from the wall. Except he wasn't accompanied by fellow officers who understood his reactions, so he needed to try harder to get his point across. He jumped up at the wall, resting his paws on it, and began digging. A few chunks of dirt fell.

"What is it, boy? You want out of here, don't you?" Helen asked as Miranda wondered if the dog's brain had been damaged from the fall into the hole.

Five feet from Beef's paws, through the soil, lay the mutilated corpse of Illinois Republican Senator Neil Hainer III.

◎　　◎　　◎

It was the largest community gathering in Shady Springs. Kensington Park was filled, curb to curb, with artist booths, food trucks, and five stages of musical entertainment. People traveled from surrounding communities to get a taste of MaPa's cabbage rolls and pierogi stuffed with mashed potatoes, jalapeno peppers, and cheddar cheese.

Neil was there on business. He was scheduled to mingle and chat about topics assigned to his general assembly committee, including agriculture, gaming, and confined animal feeding operations. The best and most appropriate place to plant himself in all the crowded craziness of the festival was the livestock exhibitions. The *baas* of the sheep and wails from the pygmy goats kept him alert as he introduced himself to the mostly uninterested people of the community. Nobody really wanted to hear about the newly added crop fields or how the price of grain had taken a nosedive, especially when deep-fried s'mores lived around the corner.

"Republicans are the worst."

Neil turned to face his sister, Ann. He laughed and hugged her.

"What are you doing here?" he asked, not having seen her since the Christmas holiday five months ago.

"Surprise!" She shared she was there to see one of her favorite independent folk bands and wanted to surprise her big brother, as she had seen on Facebook, that he was attending the festival. Neil missed seeing Ann regularly as she'd moved to Wisconsin five years ago after a family meltdown. Their brother, Neil's twin, had robbed the family of cash and valuables during a bout with sex addiction. He blew his wad on prostitutes and could not keep a job because he slept with coworkers or sexually harassed the ones who wouldn't bed him. He'd fathered two children from two different women. Their parents helped him pay child support and enabled his addiction for years until the siblings couldn't take it anymore. They were all in their twenties, post college, and living in Indiana under their parents' roof when the explosion occurred. Ann then moved to Wisconsin, and Neil moved to Chicago where he ran several small law firms before his love for politics led him to a position in the Illinois General Assembly. At age thirty, he was one of the youngest Senators in the country.

"Hi, Neil." The twin brother with all the problems walked up behind Ann.

"Carl? Hey." Neil glared at Ann who showed no signs of surprise that Carl was there. He suddenly felt ambushed. Why hadn't she warned him? Why were they there together, and when had they reconciled? "How are you?" Neil scanned Carl's body, checking for signs of sickness. His face looked fuller, and he seemed put together. His thick, brown hair was parted to the side, matching Neil's style. Not at all disheveled like the last time he had seen him two years ago in a rehabilitation facility.

"I'm wonderful. I feel great. I'm healthy, and I wanted to prove it." He held out his hand, and Neil slowly raised his own to shake.

"That's great. You're on meds that are actually working?"

"Yeah, bro." Carl chuckled. "The meds are top-notch."

"He's still in therapy as well," Ann added.

"Good. I haven't heard any reports lately, so that's good to know."

"Oh, I also want you to know that I forgive you," Carl said.

Ann pulled him back from Neil. "Look, can we save this conversation for another time, Carl?"

"Forgive me for what?"

Carl laughed. "Oh, maybe for destroying my life? How about that?"

"If you're talking about going to jail, that is all you, Carl."

"You called the fucking cops! I didn't call the cops. Mom and Dad didn't call the cops. Ann didn't call the cops. They wanted to help me with my addiction. They did what families are supposed to do, support and help me. You just wanted me gone. I was an embarrassment. You wanted me locked away and forgotten about so I couldn't ruin your shitty political career."

Neil looked at Ann. "Thanks for this. How could you possibly think this was a good idea? I'm working here. Get him away from me."

Neil turned and took a few steps before Carl spun him around and punched him in his right eye, sending him into the llama exhibit. The three large animals screamed at him as he tried to pick himself up off the hay-covered ground, their piercing screams sounding like raptors from *Jurassic Park*.

"Your days of treating me like dirt are over, Mr. Senator Hotshot!" Carl said from the broken fence above his brother as one of the screaming llamas approached. "Shut up, you ugly thing." The llama spit in Carl's face. "Fuck!" He wiped his cheek and retreated as Neil stood and started laughing.

"I'm so sorry, Neil." Ann pulled Carl away, and they disappeared into the gathering crowd.

A couple men helped Neil over the fence, and he wiped the dirt and straw from his dress slacks, striped shirt, and tie. He noticed other people in the crowd with their phones pointed at him, snapping pictures or recording video, so he quickly fled the scene. He passed an older man and an even older woman as he entered a portable restroom.

◎　　◎　　◎

"That's him," Hubert said to his mother, Loretta, as they were on their fourth capture mission that day.

"No, it ain't! He wasn't wearin' no tie." Loretta grabbed the photograph from her son. They'd been following Carl since his sister picked him up an hour ago but lost him shortly after getting to the park. They had a doozy of a time finding discreet parking for the rented van with handicap accessibility.

Little did they realize that Carl had a twin brother.

"He must've changed when we got here," Hubert offered as Loretta approached the plastic crap house. "What are you doing? Get back here!" She waved her hand at him and banged on the door. "Shit!" Hubert hid behind the trunk of a nearby chestnut tree.

"There's someone in here!" The man they suspected was Carl yelled, an annoyance clearly oozing from his voice.

"Is that you, Carl Hainer?" Loretta asked, wanting firm confirmation but not really thinking of the consequences. Little did she realize that within this portable john more than just bodily waste was being expelled.

Inside, the man not-named-Carl sat in silence, his mind spinning over the question that had just been asked. He wondered why the old lady on the outside wanted his brother.

And then he had a terrible idea. An idea that would cost him his life, but he was convinced that Carl was still up to no good and that this could be his chance of proving it and setting his sister straight. He couldn't believe she had let him back in her life. Neil needed to prove to her that their brother would never change.

"Yes. Yes, I'm Carl. Why?" Loretta turned to search for her son, thrones of people walking all around her. She spotted him peeking from behind a tree and gave him a thumbs-up. And then an obviously drunk or high teenage boy bumped into her, knocking her to her knees.

"Sorry, Granny," he said and laughed as he continued.

"Fuck off, hoodlum!" Loretta screamed as she whipped him the bird. Hubert rushed forward and helped her to her feet.

"You okay, Mama?" She nodded. Hubert was very uneasy about this TOA considering the amount of witnesses. The others had been planned a little more strategically and privately but given that they only had two days to herd these human cattle, they needed to improvise a little and Loretta was the perfect ploy. Who would suspect an eighty-year-old woman could do anything other than watch *Wheel of Fortune*?

Hubert grabbed a wheelchair hidden in a nearby bush, unfolded it, and quickly pushed it to his mama. "Get him to the van. The back side that's up against the fence so that nobody'll see. Got it?" She nodded once again and plopped onto the chair.

"Hello? You still out there?" the man yelled, Loretta barely hearing over the bass pumping from a nearby stage.

"Yes, dear."

"What is the story? What are you going to say?" Hubert asked as they heard their victim shuffling around in the plastic box. "Shit. He's wiping. I gots to go. See you soon." He kissed her cheek and hobbled off.

"I remember. Don'tcha worry!" she called after him. The outhouse door opened and out stepped the well-dressed man. "Hi, Carl."

"Hello, um…." Neil almost blew the plan and asked her name. Since she knew Carl, he should probably know who she was. "How are you? Long time no see, eh?" He nervously chuckled, instigating the pain in his right eye, which was quickly swelling from the punch.

Loretta was confused by these words since they had never met. "I was wonderin' if you'd help me to my car. My arms are played out."

"Okay. Where are you parked?"

"Just start pushin', and I'll tell ya."

Neil grabbed the handles in the back and did as he was told. People scattered as they went through the bumpy, grassy park. "How did you find me in this crowd?"

Confused, Loretta frowned. For a moment, she thought he knew the real reason she was there. "Just luck, I guess. Over thata way." She pointed. "I've got some stuff for ya."

"Fantastic. What is it?" Neil immediately regretted his word choice. He doubted Carl ever used the word *fantastic*. But would this woman even notice? He waited to hear the incriminating evidence. Which drug was it and were there other shady dealings happening? He was briefly saddened that his brother had involved this handicapped, sweet old woman in his illegal activities.

"Crack. And snatch." Loretta giggled. Maybe she wasn't so sweet after all.

"And why would you have this for me?"

"You know, dirty man. What could be hotter than a pair of crotchless panties and a briefcase full of—" Loretta flew off the wheelchair as they hit a deep hole in the field. She landed in the lap of a three-hundred-pound man stretched out on a blanket, enjoying a beer and a joint.

"Whoa, mama!" He rolled her off him, her full-length, gray, paisley dress hiking up to her waist, exposing her bloomer-less bottom half. The man's hand skimmed the woman's naked crotch. "Shit, lady, sorry." He shook his hand as if a crab had attached itself to his finger.

Neil bent and pulled her dress down, quickly trying to erase the view of wrinkly ass from his brain. He scooped her up, placed her back in the chair, and apologized to the stoner.

"Okay, let's get you out of the grass." He veered from the field onto the closest sidewalk, and they started going in a slightly different direction.

Loretta was disoriented from the fall. She had no idea where the van was parked. "Stop!" Neil froze. "Where are you taking me?"

"To your car, right? What kind of car do you drive?"

"It's a van. A white van."

Neil spotted a van up ahead. "I see it. No worries, um...." He couldn't ask her name if he knew her. "Please, tell me again what you have for me?"

"Roofies. You know, what you used to rape those women."

Neil stopped pushing, shocked and disgusted. He never knew rape was on the menu with his brother. He was even more enraged by the events of tonight. He couldn't wait to narc to his sister. He also couldn't wait to get away from this woman. The more she spilled, the less he liked her. He pushed her to the van resting across the street. She shook her head and told him it wasn't her van. She pointed in the opposite direction, and they turned and continued their expedition.

This wasn't the first time Neil had pretended to be Carl.

When they were sixteen, Carl had been grounded but wanted to see a girl he was forbidden to see. She was black, and their parents were uncomfortable with the pairing, although they refused to admit they were being racist. Fortunately, the twins had similar hairstyles but they did dress differently, so they swapped clothing, and Carl said his goodbyes to his parents, pretending to be Neil and going to a friend's house. The real Neil hid in his bedroom and read—something Carl never did—so anytime a parent came to his room he swapped the book for a video game. If Neil truly had done what Carl did all the time, he would've been jerking off all day: a harbinger of his brother's adult problems. It was difficult for Neil to imagine that he'd actually done something nice for his brother and that they'd been close at one time. That closeness seemed lifetimes ago.

"Maybe that way." Neil's passenger pointed, and he pushed her down the sidewalk that separated the parked cars from a row of large houses facing the park. "A bunch of rich assholes live here," she said as they passed the homes.

Several groups of younger adults passed them on their way to the end of the dead-end street. Another white van was indeed parked in the very last spot. No house faced the van, just the backside of a convenience store.

It was definitely private enough—the perfect spot for an abduction.

"You drive this van yourself?" Neil asked and then had a moment of alarm, forgetting he should probably know the answer. He pushed her to the driver's door and reached for the handle.

"Push me around back, please. That's how I load myself in," Loretta requested, and he grabbed her chair and pushed her around the back, dropping from the sidewalk onto the street rather abruptly.

"Damnit, Carl. You already dropped me on the ground. You're pretty fucking careless."

Neil chuckled, as he thought it funny to hear the old woman curse. He also thought it was funny when young children cursed, something he never shared when running for senator. "Where's my stuff?"

"Inside." Loretta pointed to the back door. "Open it and jump in."

"Bullshit. I'm not going inside." He'd seen enough movies to know better. You don't just jump into a mysterious van, especially when you know the owner of the van is involved in illegal activities. Also, as a politician, you just don't do stupid shit. The only reason he was even in the situation was to prove his brother was still a douchebag.

Loretta kicked his left shin. He screamed.

"Why'd you do that?" She kicked him again, and he fell to his knees. The back door to the van opened above his head, and Hubert jumped out and shoved a syringe into Neil's back. Hubert's knees gave out, and he landed on his on his ass. Neil screamed again. "What the fuck?" He reached around and pulled the needle out of his back and threw it into a nearby boxwood. He then stood, as did Hubert, who pushed him into the van.

There were three other unconscious bodies lying inside. Neil scrambled to his feet, banging his head on the roof of the van as he turned to the back doors. Hubert slammed them and locked them from the outside.

The anesthetic raced through Neil's blood, and he became lightheaded. He fell back, the white walls resembling the inside of a twister as they spun wildly. He tried to look for an escape, but there was no way out. The front seats were on the other side of a thick metal wall and screen. His thoughts of escape faded as his legs turned to cooked spaghetti and he collapsed onto his stomach. He propped his head up long enough to see a young girl. Was she dead? Was he dying? Those were his last two thoughts as blackness engulfed him.

◉　◉　◉

"Just push 'em down there. They'll be okay," Loretta instructed her son. They had the van backed up to the landfill. The four unconscious passengers were the first of the kidnapped to arrive at their new luxurious home of trash.

"No, Mama! You heard the man. He wants them alive, or it's our asses. And we get zero cash. You hear me? Zero fuckin' cash. That defeats the whole purpose of this shit." Hubert wished he hadn't filled in the ramp that led to the bottom of the hole with dirt and clay years earlier. Of course, he would've never guessed he'd be throwing humans down there.

"Where's that rope?" Loretta asked.

His original plan was to lower them down with a rope, but how would he get them untied once they hit the ground? He needed an alternate plan and fast before Loretta ran out of steam. He had been tempted to ask his brother for help but decided he didn't want to share the money. The super-sized doses of anesthesia drugs were supposed to keep them out for seventy-two hours, which should be more than enough time to get them into the hole.

"Rope won't work."

"A ladder, Sonny?"

"Not long enough."

"For crying, fuck's sake. You didn't think of this when you agreed to do this? What that man tell you?"

"Not to kill them. Not to use rope cause they'd climb out with it."

"They ain't dying if you put them in gently. There's enough water and trash to break their fall, Sonny." It had rained the night before, and water lifted the trash. "Just try one. The girl."

Hubert opened the two back doors of the van and pulled out the wheelchair. Helen, Mia, Byron, and Neil were sleeping peacefully, although they had shifted a bit on the ride, and Helen's head rested in Byron's crotch. Hubert grabbed Helen's foot and pulled her. She easily slid on the metal floor of the van. When she got to the edge, he navigated her body to fall into the wheelchair. Minimal stress and strain for the girl and for the old man with chronic pain in his knees and back. He pushed the wheelchair to the edge of the hole and peered down.

It was quite a drop. His fear of heights made him queasy. "I don't know about this, Mama."

Loretta walked to the edge and looked down as well. "Lotsa trash down there, Sonny. It'll break her fall."

Hubert turned back to the van for a moment, time enough for his eighty-year-old mother to tip the wheelchair and send the girl flying.

"Holy shit!" Hubert muttered as Helen landed on her back, free from death. The bags of trash acted as balloons, and the few feet of rancid water cushioned the impact, creating a tiny splash.

"Never doubt your mama. I mean, come on! I raised you into the upstanding man you are today. I think you can trust me." She smiled and swatted Hubert's arm. "Next!" They pushed the wheelchair back to the van and looked at the body pile.

Neil was gone.

"Fuck a duck," Loretta elegantly stated as her panic-stricken, upstanding son hobbled around the van, looking for the escapee.

"I don't see him. I don't see him!" They both made their way to the front of the van, facing out to the mixture of field and woods. No movement caught their eyes. "How could he disappear so fast?"

"Maybe he's like that invisible guy from the movies. He just snaps his fingers and turns invisible." Loretta laughed.

"This isn't funny! You want to go to jail for kidnappin'? Huh? And what the hell movie did that ever happen in?" A moan sounded from nearby. "Shh." They walked to the opened rear of the van. The two bodies inside were motionless.

Neil rolled out from underneath the van and stood before he was spotted.

"What do ya think you're doin'?" Hubert asked.

"Where am I? What's happening?" Neil slurred as he fell to his knees, trying to fight off the drug running through his blood.

"Get another shot," Hubert told Loretta as he walked to Neil. "Come on, you're not going anywhere." Hubert tried to stand him up, but Neil's six-foot, two-hundred-pound body wouldn't cooperate. Loretta appeared with a large syringe.

"No!" Neil mustered enough strength to stand. Hubert grabbed his arm, and they struggled. Neil broke free and stumbled toward the landfill, unaware it even existed until it was practically under him. "What the fuck is this?"

Loretta shoved the needle into his back and pumped him with the sleep serum. He still had a little fight, as he turned and swung at Hubert, missing him by a yard. Hubert then ran at him with full force and shoved him.

Neil glided through the air gracefully, arms outstretched, like a hawk searching for its next meal. The second dose of anesthesia kicked in mid-flight and rendered him unconscious once again, which spared him the pain of his death. He landed in the middle of the landfill, a broken broomstick impaling his neck, severing his carotid artery and sending a spray of blood into the air.

"We're fucked," Loretta said.

After the blood geyser subsided, Neil's body sank under a pile of rubbish.

"He can't be seen. We'll play dumb. Maybe he'll be okay anyways."

"You won't need to play dumb, Sonny. You are dumb. That dude is dead with a capital *D*."

For a moment, Hubert was disturbed. Although he had seen a few dead men, he had never killed a man. He eventually justified it by concluding it wasn't his fault. It was the luck of the draw, or in this case, the fall. They carried on with their task of unloading the remaining victims, dropping them into other safe-looking areas below. Although the drops weren't always graceful, no more blood geysers erupted. Another day and another set of victims and they would await the visit from the man with the one million dollars in cash. The property and the landfill would be his, and Hubert and his mother would head to Hawaii, their remaining days spent in the sun and the sand.

◙　　◙　　◙

The first night, while the unconscious bodies soaked in filth, Neil's body was dragged into a tunnel hidden in the wall of the landfill. The creature that only Miranda believed existed feasted on Neil's right arm. The same arm Neil had raised when he was sworn in as Senator of the United States.

THE LIGHT

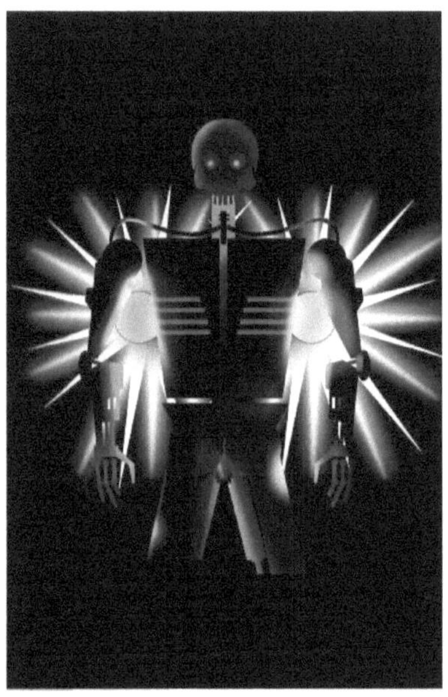

Everyone sat on their tires as the last bit of light vanished. Beef had given up on uncovering human remains when he realized his dog nails couldn't damage the wall of clay. Miranda found her weapon against the beast she feared would reappear: a blood-stained, broken broomstick. Glen sat as still as possible. Each movement caused his gunshot wound to throb in pain, and he couldn't take the intolerant stares or snickers when he squealed.

A somber silence engulfed the group. They were all lost in their heads, fearing the worst. "He keeps the feet of His godly ones, but the wicked ones are silenced in darkness; For not by might shall a man prevail," Father Daniel preached.

"Anything more upbeat?" Colin asked.

"We are wicked? Is that what you're saying, Priest? Well, you must be too, then." Miranda crawled out of the shelter and stood facing the location of the beast the night before. She held the broomstick tightly. "Come get us!" she screamed into the blackness. Beef left the camp to investigate. He stood next to Miranda. "You'll warn us, won't you, boy?" He barked. Helen also joined them.

"Again, how would Bigfoot get in and out of here?" Glen yelled and winced in pain.

"Don't worry about it," Miranda said. "I'll protect you all. I'll kill this monster. The son of a bitch followed me here from under my bed. He murdered my dad."

"Somebody has lost their mind," Glen said, and it was partially true. The lack of food on what would be day number five—three unconscious, two awake—was enough to cause hallucinations and cognitive dysfunction.

"Are we going to wither away to nothing down here? Is that how we're going to die?" Mia asked anyone who was listening, which was everyone. What else was there to do but listen in the decaying black hole? Fasting was not new to Mia, but the longest she'd gone without food to prepare for an audition or a role in a film was three days. But she always drank lots of fluids.

"We're getting out of here tomorrow. One way or another," Colin said with conviction. He needed to not only convince the others but himself as well.

"Okay, but if not, we need to eat. We need to eat that dog," Glen suggested to the moans and disapproval of the others on the tires. "Fine. I'll eat him myself."

"We're getting out of here tomorrow, Glen. My boyfriend needs me," Colin said, outing himself to those who didn't already suspect. He then shared the story of the nightclub shooting. The others knew nothing of it. They had been abducted prior to that event.

"I'm so sorry. That's horrible," Mia said.

"I will say a prayer for your lover and your people," Daniel said, stirring a groan in Colin.

"He's my boyfriend. Lover is so retro. We are allowed to be in committed relationships, you know: us gays. And they're not my people. They're people, period. We deserve the same rights as anyone else. But I'm not getting into political bullshit. It's not my thing."

"You're not a stereotype. I would've never guessed you liked the hard salami." Glen laughed and then screamed in pain.

"And I don't feel one bit sorry for you right now, Glen. You just made it easy on me."

"You wouldn't believe how many closeted actors are out there. It's the strangest thing to see them hanging on set with their significant others but never acknowledging it, even though everyone on the production knows. And it's amazing it never leaks to the press," said Mia.

"It's all about spinning the story, even if it gets out. Unless you have a sex tape or pics of salami sucking, it'll never stick," Glen said carefully, trying to avoid more pain.

"Please stop talking about salami. My stomach is crying right now. It's going to start eating my lungs," Colin said.

"Since you're a nurse and you know these things, what happens when you starve to death?" The question they all thought about at least once that day came out of Father Daniel's mouth.

"Well, as you said, I'm a nurse, not a doctor, but I have a little experience with starvation. And we had studies on it as well. Your body basically eats itself."

"So, you weren't joking when you said your stomach wants to eat your lungs?"

"Well, kinda. That is the final stage. When your organs shut down. Your body will burn through your fat first. Then muscle."

"How long?"

"That's the good thing here. Someone who has more fat will survive longer. But we have weeks of no food. It's a lengthy, painful process. But lack of water and dehydration—that'll do you in much sooner. We're talking a week or less of no water."

"And we have no idea how long we've been out here," said Mia.

"Starvation and dehydration are probably less of a threat right now than injury and infection. Anyone who has a substantial injury, torn or ripped flesh, is exposed to the filth down here. It doesn't take long to develop an infection."

"How long?" Glen asked, panic in his voice.

"Seconds to get infected, but symptoms don't show for a day or so."

"Okay, I'm feeling nauseous. Let's stop talking about this."

"We need water. Most important. Rain would be a blessing. We should've captured some last night."

"The only thing that got captured last night was Byron." Miranda was closer to the dwelling now. "If he were still here, we would've found him today. He was nowhere to be found."

"Okay. Maybe Bigfoot can fly. That would be fucking great! He can fly us the hell out of here!"

"That's okay, Glen. I'm saving my energy to kill this thing, not to scream at you. Or call you a piece of shit for screwing everything that walks. Yeah, that's right, I heard it all. But I'm not getting upset. I'm saving my energy; you piece of shit." Miranda stepped away again.

"Way to hold back."

"Are you okay, Miranda?" Helen asked when she returned to her side.

"Yes, my little buddy. And I mean that sincerely, don't start pissing and moaning about being little. You need to enjoy being young while you can."

"I know. My grandma tells me that all the time."

"Well, hello! Grandmas are the shit! They know everything! I wish your grandma was here right now. She'd tell us how to get out of here and how to kill this monster!"

"She would. I wish she was here too. I miss her." Emotion took over, and Helen cried. She hated crying and usually had control over it, but in her current weakened state she couldn't keep it locked inside.

"It's okay, sweetie. You'll be seeing her soon." Miranda pressed the girl close to her.

"I treat her so bad. She should hate my guts. I'm so mean to her." Helen continued to weep.

"You know, that's what grandchildren do. Grandchildren are the shits, but differently, but that's okay, you know? Kids don't listen to elders, they think they know it all. It's normal. Don't beat yourself up over it. Your Grams knows you love her." Helen squeezed Miranda's waist as the mother of three caressed her hair and rubbed her back.

"Shh. Listen," Daniel said.

Everyone stopped moving or talking. A faint crunching sounded from above. The crunching of stones under tires. And then a pair of headlights appeared over them, reaching from one side of the hole to the other.

"Help!"

"Down here!"

Two car doors slammed, and two figures appeared, blocking the bridge of light. The light from behind them projected their figures, creating giant shadows reminiscent of the Batman signal in the sky. Only these shadows weren't there to serve and protect or to fight crime.

"Help!" Everyone was on their feet, waving their unseen hands and screaming. Except for Punam, of course. She was being consumed by the infection Colin had warned them about moments before.

"Helen Redfield," a cyborg warrior voice from above shouted through a voice-altering megaphone. "Are you down there, Helen?"

"Yes! I'm here!"

"Glen Hampton, meteorologist, are you down there?" the cyborg warrior asked as several of the sewer rats believed they were in a sequel to *The Terminator*.

"Yes," Glen said and bit his tongue to ease the pain. "Please get me out of here! I've been shot!" His request was ignored.

"Miranda Lambert? Oops, sorry, I meant Lassort. Not the hot piece of country music trash." The cyborg chuckled.

"Yes. I'm Miranda Lassort. What the fuck is going on here? Get us out of here!" They quickly surmised the figures above weren't there to save them.

"Priest Daniel?"

"Father Daniel. Yes, I am down here."

"Punam Shetty." Silence. "Punam? Punam?"

"She's wounded. Unconscious. Near death. She needs medical attention right now!" Colin yelled, hoping their captor would show a little pity.

"Colin Danielson?" The cyborg voice continued its roll call.

"That's me."

"Mia Philly, needing a willy." The cyborg laughed.

"I'm here. Please get us out of here!"

"Byron Baxtor?"

"He was attacked and taken by a big, hairy creature," Miranda said.

"Taken where?"

"We don't know. It was dark and rainy. They just vanished."

"Bullshit. Did he escape?" Cyborg man sounded slightly panicked.

"We think he was killed," Miranda said.

The figures retreated from view, and the headlights shone brightly across the hole once again.

"What is happening here? Why is this guy disguising his voice? It's someone we all know or an actor whose voice we can recognize," said Glen. He then realized how ridiculous that sounded. "It's someone we know or someone we know. Why else would he disguise his voice?"

The shadows reappeared, and the roll call continued. "Carl Hainer?" The group looked around at one another's slightly illuminated and puzzled faces. "Carl Hainer?"

"No, Carl Hainer down here."

"Did the hairy creature get him too?" the voice sarcastically asked.

"We never saw him." Another pause and the shadows once again retreated. Car doors were opened and closed, and the vehicle backed away from the opening.

"No! Don't leave us!" Mia begged.

Helen and Miranda also started yelling up. Fifteen seconds later, the lights disappeared, and the crunching gravel faded to a dead silence.

◉　　◉　　◉

"I don't know what they're talking about. Carl and Brian are down there, I swear to you!" Hubert told the man driving the black Lexus.

"His name is Byron. And you aren't getting a lick of cash from me until those two turn up."

The man wore a black newsboy cap, but he was far from a boy's age. Hubert guessed they were the same age. Thick, black-rimmed glasses and a large overcoat completed his look. He was not only trying to disguise his voice but also his appearance. This was only the second time Hubert had seen him: the first time was daylight two weeks earlier, but he was once again wearing the cap and sunglasses that covered his entire face.

This unnamed man had showed up on Hubert's property and invited himself inside the cottage. He had a business proposition that would reward Hubert and his mother handsomely, but the work would be tough. If they pulled it off, financial reward would be theirs for the rest of their lives. The man also indicated he could easily get Hubert jail time for the illegal dumping, as well as other shady dealings, if he didn't cooperate. Hubert wasn't sure how this man knew about the other dealings, but he wasn't pressing for information. He agreed to the terms, and the man arranged everything: the TOAs, the locations, the van, and the sleeping drugs. He also provided photos of the soon-to-be abductees.

"I think Carl is dead. I'm sorry. He fell, and there was blood, and he didn't move again. I think he's buried down there." The man turned his head to Hubert, and he assumed the man was unhappy, but he couldn't tell with his disguise. "I swear on my mama's life. If I'm lying, I will watch you slit her throat like you do a hog. Shit, I'll even help."

They pulled up to the cottage.

"Find Byron then. Confirm he isn't on his way to the police. Keep in mind there is no evidence I exist or have any involvement with any of this, so you will be the one incarcerated and spending the rest of your life in prison, getting your tired, wrinkled anus violated repeatedly until you can't walk. I'll be back tomorrow to begin the proceedings." Hubert sat quietly in the passenger seat. "Okay, you can get out now. You think I stopped here to share pleasantries or to bond with you? Exit my vehicle immediately!"

Hubert left the car, and the man sped away on the long, winding gravel road.

◉　　◉　　◉

Back in the shithole, the sewer rats had renewed hope. The fact that someone had showed up made them feel less isolated. Even though that someone was a confirmed enemy, there was still hope they could get out of the dump. They pondered the identity of the dark man from above and how they all connected to him.

A high-pitched scream erupted from Punam, followed by rapid convulsions for a handful of seconds and then stillness.

"I think that was her last breath," Father Daniel stated.

Colin crawled over and attempted to resuscitate her. A minute of pumping passed without a hint of breath.

"Don't you have last rites or something you can be saying now? Pray!" Colin screamed in frustration as he continued his attempt at revival.

"O Lord Jesus Christ, most merciful, Lord of earth, we ask that you receive this child into your arms, that he might pass—"

"She!"

"Yes, sorry—that *she* might pass in safety from this crisis. As thou hast told us with infinite compassion."

Punam awakened in bed next to her husband. The morning light exploded into the bedroom through the white, sheer curtains. She felt amazing. No hangover or disorientation about what had happened the night before.

"Good morning, beautiful," Gerald greeted. They were lying on their sides, facing one another. He kissed

her. Why was he being nice to her? They barely spoke to each other, and he hadn't complimented her in ages.

"Let not your heart be troubled: ye believe in God, believe also in me."

Colin was administering mouth-to-mouth. The group stood in a circle around the action, just outside the covered shelter. There was enough moonlight above to see what was happening.

Gerald pulled his lips away from Punam and smiled. He caressed her bare shoulder. "I love you," he whispered. She felt protected—safe from physical and emotional harm. The warm sunlight on her cheek and her husband's soft touch soothed her. She closed her eyes and quietly sighed.

"By this sign thou art anointed with the grace of the atonement of Jesus Christ and thou art, um, thou art…" Father Daniel fumbled with his last rites as Colin turned Punam on her side and asked for help to keep her in that position as he hit her back, hoping not to open her wounds anymore. "Thou art absolved of all past error and freed to take your place in the world he has prepared for us."

"Mommy!" Three-year-old Alecia stood in the doorway of the bedroom, elated to see her mother in the bed next to her father. Punam's eyes flew open, and she studied Gerald's face, her back to the door. Gerald smiled and nodded. Punam rolled over and faced the doorway and the daughter she barely knew. Alecia had Punam's thick, dark hair, which was shoulder length. She was wearing SpongeBob SquarePants pajamas, a

cartoon her infant eyes always widened for when it was on the television.

"Alecia?" How did this happen? Why didn't she know her daughter had returned?

Punam approached Alecia, kneeled in front of her, slowly took her into her arms, and softly squeezed, afraid she'd break her bones if she hugged as tightly as she wanted. She pulled away after a very long minute and took in Alecia's beauty. And then the tidal wave of tears burst from her eyes as she pulled her daughter against her body once again.

"And thus, do I commend thee into the arms of our lord of earth, our Lord Jesus Christ, preserver of all mercy and reality, and the father creator."

Colin placed Punam on her back once again. Minutes had passed and still no breath of life. Her body was cold. There was nothing more he could do.

"It's time to come with me, Mommy," Alecia said. Punam pulled away from her once again and stared into her eyes, realization setting in that this wasn't happening in the real world. She turned back to the bed, and it was no longer there. Her husband was gone as well. "It's okay, Mommy. I've been waiting for you. I was sad when I got here, but he told me I would get to see you soon, so that made me happy."

"I'm happy too, baby. I've been waiting for this moment for so long." Punam stood and turned around, the bedroom gradually fading into white. Her daughter took her hand.

"Come, Mommy." They began walking into the light she originally thought was the morning sun. Punam now knew this was the light of anointment. The light of love, forgiveness, comfort, redemption, and reconciliation. Her smile widened until it was consumed by the radiance.

"We give him glory as we give you into his arms in everlasting peace."

THE DARK

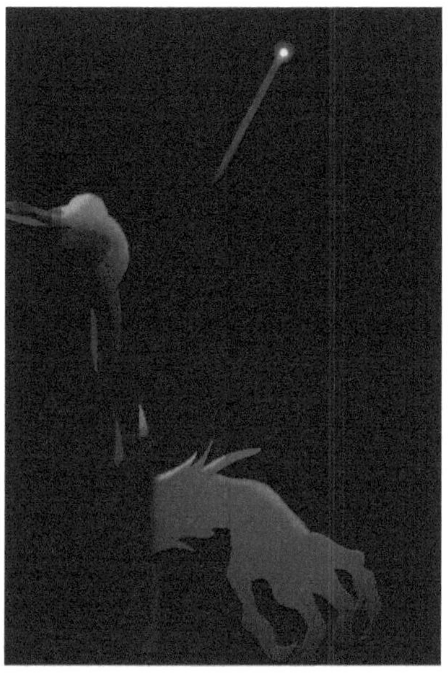

He coughed up a ball of dust or dirt; he wasn't sure what it was because he was in complete darkness. Not a hint of light. No iris adjustment to help him see the tiniest of outlines. Awakening in this fashion was becoming a bad habit he wanted to quit. Unfortunately, quitting was beyond his control.

Byron recalled the rain and lightning and the ivory-furred creature with the emerald-green eyes. The creature had bonked him on the head, which dazed him but didn't completely knock him out. He felt himself being dragged under a makeshift pile of debris. Beneath the debris was a hole that seemed barely large enough to squeeze both of their bodies through, especially the massive beast.

It was also the entryway to a tunnel that led to freedom.

Byron was unaware of the freedom potential, but the journey through this tunnel would be difficult for the amateur. For the creature, which resembled a cross between Bigfoot and the Abominable Snowman, it was a manageable crawl from the entrance in the landfill to the exit fifty feet above in the thick woods. The exit of the hole was covered by a heavy rug of twigs, and the tunnel was on an incline approximately a quarter of a mile, with a larger, excavated opening in the middle used as the creature's living quarters. This was the current location of Byron. He was in an upright position against the interior wall of dirt. His wrists were secured by exposed tree roots, and his feet were tied by a rope.

"Hello!" he yelled, stirring another spitball of earth.

He wiggled his tied hands, each stretched as far to his sides as his arms could extend. The knots weren't loosening. He stopped struggling and strained his ears to pick up a movement of any kind. The silence was deafening, almost like the times he wore noise-reducing headphones to drown out his girlfriend, Margarita. Maybe if he hadn't evicted her from his ears, he would've had a clue she was going to narc him out, an action that landed him in the big house and then the halfway house and then the shithouse in the ground. If he made it out of this predicament, he would pay Margarita a visit. She needed a lesson in dating etiquette.

He felt a slight temperature change on his exposed shin, as his polyester restaurant pants were ripped at the knees. It took him a moment to realize his skin was being caressed by air. An ever-so-slight movement of air entered his prison, which meant freedom wasn't too far away. He frantically pulled his wrists, feeling a bit of give, the roots not extremely thick. After a minute, though, he became winded. The lack of oxygen halted him for a moment.

And then he heard something approaching.

It was the beast. Its matted, stained fur rubbed against Byron's body, and the smell was putrid, a mixture of rotten ground beef, underarm odor, and vomit after a hard night of drinking and pizza-eating. Its breathing was labored. Byron could hear every nuance of the inhale, and the exhale was guttural. It sniffed his ear and then shuffled away. Little did Byron know that the beast was heading back down the tunnel, back to the unfortunate senator—the man he was eating—near the hole to the landfill.

◉   ◉   ◉

The beast was named Rocka, shortened from the Rocket Mile Monster. He had been named decades ago when spotted a half-dozen times in Rocket Mile State

Park, fifty miles south of Shady Hill. Moving proved difficult for him without being discovered, and the park wasn't thickly wooded. Every one of his former homes in the neighboring forests turned up a hunter or five, scaring Rocka into the next park. He finally ceased his relocations when he stumbled upon the Carlyle Dump, conveniently, at the time Hubert was filling in the ramp to the landfill. The soil was the perfect consistency to easily dig a tunnel and make a home underground where he could live undetected. The first four years in his new home were the easiest living of his sixty-three-year life. His food came daily as deer and other wildlife fell into his tunnel. When it came time to hunt, he simply swapped out the heavy twig tunnel cover for a lighter, mostly leafy one that was easier for the wildlife to fall through. If he weren't so hairy and scary, he could get a patent for this contraption.

◙　　◙　　◙

Rocka peeled a layer of skin from Neil's thigh and shoved it in his mouth. It was tough and chewy, but he had the razor-sharp teeth required to break it down into swallowable pieces. His next feast was hanging in his lair, and he didn't want to get overzealous and kill him before he could finish this meal. He needed to keep his food fresh, as he didn't have the luxury of a freezer. Also, he didn't know what a freezer was, although he'd seen a few of them in the landfill. Maneuvering in the blackness of the tunnel was challenging, and he relied on his sensitive sense of smell to guide him, although his eyes did adjust slightly to allow the faintest of vision.

He ripped a chunk of muscle this time. As he was shredding it, he caught a whiff of a recently deceased human coming from the landfill. He stood alert. This could be his next meal. It smelled of the female persuasion, and it had been a while since he had eaten a woman. This was more of a dessert. Sweet and tender. He jumped five feet to the bottom of the tunnel, which then curved up to the hidden exit.

It was time to infiltrate his smorgasbord.

He crawled out from under the trash and slowly stood. His eyes zoomed in on the covered camp. Shadows moved around. He heard a female crying as he watched several humans gently place his future dinner away from the camp.

Rocka's goal was to grab the fresh meat and disappear back into the tunnel without the others noticing. He'd discovered many years ago that his eyesight in the dark was much better than a human's. He knew what he could get away with, at least when a canine wasn't nearby. Those loud noisemakers put a crimp in his style. He was prepared to kill anyone or anything that interfered with his mission.

He took a big step forward, his target about thirty feet away. He heard chatter.

"I've never seen a dead body before," a female said.

"Good thing it's dark then," a male muttered.

Rocka couldn't understand the human language, only voice tones. He understood emotions and facial expressions as well, but it usually didn't matter. He wasn't spending time with this species to understand them or communicate with them. He wanted to eat them. He needed them for nourishment when food was scarce. Otherwise, the deer and the raccoons and the squirrels were enough.

He took two more rapid steps and paused to decipher if he'd been detected. He was safe.

A throng of rats rushed by, squeaking at each other. They ran past the human's camp, prompting a shriek from one of the ladies. The dog chased after them, leaving the camp area.

Now was the beast's chance. He made several large leaps; the barking disguised the rustling of the trash under his large feet. He paused again. Nobody screamed or ran from him or tried to attack him, so he was still undetected.

"Something foul smelling this way comes!" the man in the robe cried, pointing in Rocka's direction. All eyes shifted, and a woman rose with her broomstick. This was the tone that informed the beast he'd been discovered.

Rocka screeched, and it sounded alien in pitch. This was his first line of defense to scare humans away. The group crawled out of their shelter and backed away; everyone but the woman with the weapon. She ran at the beast, her broomstick spear pointed at him. Rocka pulled his arm back in anticipation, like a baseball pitcher winding up for a pitch, and when she arrived at his perimeter of space, he swung his large arm and swatted the woman away. She flew into a nearby trash pile, her broomstick taking flight and landing even farther away.

Rocka took three more large steps, scooped Punam into his arms, and then quickly retreated into darkness. He threw the woman's lifeless body into the hole and then jumped in himself, landing on her chest, his huge weight crushing her ribs. He dragged her up the tunnel and dropped her on the other side of Neil. He liked to keep his food supply separated. He didn't want the old to contaminate the new.

He made his way back up the tunnel to check on his prisoner. He would keep the man alive for a few more days until he finished the other two. When he arrived at his living quarters, he inched forward to perform his normal sniff test of his prisoner to ensure he was still breathing. He smelled soil.

The man was gone.

THE COTTAGE

Hubert settled in his old, ripped recliner with his plastic cup of bottom-shelf whiskey and his television remote. He was concerned over the two missing men, but there was nothing he could do in the dark. He would rise with the sun to investigate the landfill and its inhabitants. Knowing that he had placed the men in the hole eased his mind. He could lie about the death of whom he believed to be Carl, and Byron was surely down there somewhere, possibly dead as well. It would be important to convince the mystery man that they had died on their own if he wanted his money. He was still annoyed that Pecker had escaped his fence through a hidden hole dug behind his doghouse. This was total betrayal, and he would kill the dog when he had the chance.

Before Hubert could turn on his generic, nineteen-inch boob tube, a burst of pounding on his front door startled the shit out of him. He quickly stood and grabbed his shotgun from the kitchen counter and then slowly approached the door.

"Help!"

Hubert pulled the curtain and saw the face of one of the missing men glowing under the porch light. He smiled and giggled a little at how easy this had turned out. His stress vanished as he put on a straight face and opened the door.

The man named Byron rushed in, saw the shotgun, and raised his arms in the air. "Hey, buddy, you've got to help. There's a group of people stuck in a landfill somewhere up here."

"What's that, boy?" Hubert directed him to the couch, the shotgun pointed at him. Byron sat; his hands still raised in the air. "Put your hands down, son. I ain't gonna shoot you." He couldn't if he wanted the money and a new life.

"Look, I know this is going to sound strange, but I just escaped from a tunnel. A tunnel that must be connected to the landfill somehow. I don't remember how I got there because a large monster knocked me out and dragged me away from the others."

Hubert laughed. "Boy, what are you on? Joints? Heroin?" Hubert was naturally good at playing dumb. He wanted to ease the man down to the point of relaxation, and then he would knock him out yet again and drag him back to the hole.

The monster story was strange, though.

"No, I swear it's true. Some fucked-up shit is going on. Can we hop in your car? Better yet, you have a phone here?"

"Calm down. You want some water? Take a breath, and we'll figure this thing out." Byron nodded and leaned back on the grubby couch, his muddy and stained clothing adding to the grubbiness. Hubert filled a blue plastic cup with tap water and handed it to Byron. He drank it down in two seconds. "Another?" Hubert grabbed the cup and refilled it.

"I have no fucking idea how long I've been in that hole. This is—I don't know what to say about it—like a dream or something. Makes no sense."

Byron looked like he was ready to cry as Hubert handed him the second full cup of water. He chugged that down as well. Hubert was thinking of how perfect it would've been if he had a drug to drop in the water to knock him out. The syringes of anesthesia were all used.

Byron stood. "Okay. I'm good. Where's your phone?"

Hubert pointed the shotgun at him again. "Sit down, son." Byron sat down immediately. "How do I know you ain't talking hogwash?"

"I'm not. I—"

"How do I know you ain't here to rob me? To take all my shit?"

Byron looked around the cottage. Everything was dilapidated and cruddy: piles of clothes and boxes in the corner, kitchen counters cluttered with dirty pots and pans and glasses, and half an inch of dust coating the glass coffee table and practically every other object in sight.

"Are you serious, man? No offense, but this place is a shithole."

"Excuse me? I know it ain't as clean as it should be, but I've seen worse. You ever seen that show called *Hoarders*?"

"Yeah, I have. That's what this place reminds me of."

Hubert stepped toward Byron, aiming the shotgun at his head. "For someone who needs help, you got a strange way of askin' for it."

Byron raised his hand in front of his face. "Look, I'm sorry. C'mon, please, let me use your phone."

A door off to the right of the couch creaked open, and Loretta walked in wearing only a G-string, her tits down to her knees, rubbing her eyes. "What the fuck is all the ruckus?"

Byron looked at the mostly naked old woman and then spun away, embarrassed. And then after a quick confused expression he turned and stared hard at her face. The confused look turned to one of understanding. Hubert gathered the man had figured it out.

Byron clenched his fists. "What the fuck is going on here?"

"What is he doing here?" Loretta asked.

"Ma, go put some fucking clothes on. Jesus Christ!"

"She's your mother? You kidnapped me?"

"Don't you fuckin' move, buddy, or I'll blow your fuckin' brains out the backside of your fuckin' head."

"Sonny, why is he in here?"

"Go back to bed, Ma. I'm handling this!"

Bryon sat back, the shotgun a foot from his face. Staring down the barrel of a gun. This was a position he'd been in before, the first time being twenty-five years ago.

◎　　◎　　◎

"Hey, good morning, buddy!" Byron hugged Vincent, his best friend and roommate, relieved they had spoken the night before about life and the future over a couple of juicy burgers on the back patio while stoned as hell. Vincent had discovered Byron was in cahoots with their neighbors. They stole electronics and sold them to pawn shops or placed ads online or in newspapers. The three of them also sold drugs. But Byron was done with this. Their talk fixed him. He would find a respectable job and leave the world of crime behind.

"I think I'm never smoking pot again," Vincent concluded as he poured coffee into his mug. "I feel like shit today, and I have a feeling I made a jackass of myself with Buck and Lina."

"Lisa. Buck and Lisa."

"Yeah, right. And you're having three-ways with them? That's whack."

"Man, they're fun. But I'm done with them. I'm on the straight and narrow now, my friend."

"Okay. Let me know how the talk goes. I'll see you tonight." Vincent walked down the hall to the door, but Byron raced after him and hugged him again. "Okay, Byron, give it up. I'm not making it a four-way."

"I just wanted to thank you for understanding and not kicking me to the curb. I will change. I'll make you proud," Byron said, and it occurred to him that this was something he probably wanted to say to his father. Vincent had made it clear he really didn't want to be Byron's father figure but solely his best friend. Vincent hugged him back and said goodbye again and left.

Two minutes after the door closed, the doorbell rang.

"Good morning, Byron. Ready for some action?" Buck asked as he and Lisa entered.

"Um, what kind of action?"

"Not sex, love. You know we're not morning people," Lisa lied. Just a week ago, Byron had joined them in bed after his morning energy drink.

They walked into the living room and touched things. Attitude oozed from them; body language didn't lie.

"You think we're fuckin' idiots, don't you?" Buck reached behind his back, pulled out a gun, and shoved it into Byron's nose.

"What the fuck, dude?"

"We aren't deaf. We heard you talking to your asshole roommate last night. You don't just walk away from us," Lisa whispered in his ear as she caressed the barrel of the gun. "We got a big meeting today, and you're coming with us. Things are getting bigger."

"Look, why can't I say enough is enough? I want to work at Kentucky Fried Chicken."

"I'll Kentucky fry your dick, Byron." Buck pushed the gun into his cheek. "You think the main dude is going to let you walk? He'll fucking kill all of us. I won't let that happen. I'll kill you first."

"Fuck! Okay, get that outta my face!" Byron slowly pushed Buck's hand away. "I'm still in. But I'm getting a job at KFC too, otherwise Vincent will know I'm still working with you. Please keep it discreet."

"You're lucky I didn't kill him. The verdict is still out since you flapped your gums to him."

"I didn't tell him anything specific. Please, leave him alone. He's a great guy."

"Don't be cheating on us with him." Lisa started rubbing his dick. Byron got an erection, and they had morning sex on Vincent's couch.

The meeting later confirmed that Byron could never walk away from the seedy world of crime, as his buddy, Vincent, would later discover and finally kick him to the curb.

◎ ◎ ◎

Loretta dragged her saggy ass back into the bedroom and slammed the door, causing the mounted deer antlers above the door to fall to the floor. Hubert continued to point the shotgun at Byron's head as he planned his next step. He had to figure out a way to get him safely back to the hole, but he knew this Byron guy wouldn't go voluntarily.

"Why did you kidnap me? What could you possibly want from me or the other assholes in that hole? And what do you plan to do with us?"

"It ain't my place to answer that question."

"Questions. There were three."

"Shut your smartass mouth, fella. You ain't too bright, are ya?" Hubert stepped closer. "How did you get out of there anyways?"

"A tun—ah, I mean a rope. We found a rope and threw it out. It caught on a tree. The others are probably all out and headed to the police by now."

Hubert cracked Byron on the side of his head with the wooden shotgun stock. Byron face-dove into the cushion and stayed down. Blood trickled from his ear.

"Lying piece of shit. You said you came out of a tunnel. That ain't good either. Wake up!" Hubert kicked his leg. Byron moaned. "Get up!" He kicked him again. "You're takin' me to this tunnel."

Hubert grabbed a coil of rope. He placed the shotgun on the television and leaned in to tie Byron's hands. While he was reaching for his right hand, Byron sat up and swung his arm, his fist contacting Hubert's nose, sending him into the glass coffee table. It shattered under his weight. A broken piece of glass entered his abdomen.

"You mother—" Hubert screamed in pain as he tried to get back on his feet. The glass sticking out of his body.

Byron grabbed the shotgun and pointed it at Hubert. "Where are your car keys, huh? Your fucking phone?"

Hubert continued to sit up, but the pain was excruciating. Byron bent over and felt the front of Hubert's jean pockets but discovered nothing like keys or a phone.

And then a ringtone sounded from the kitchen counter. It was the theme song from the long-running, Western television series *Gunsmoke*, Hubert's favorite show of all time. Byron held the shotgun with his right hand as he reached for the phone with his left, his back to Loretta's bedroom door, which was slowly opening, the *Gunsmoke* theme muffling the creaking sound.

"Hello?" Byron answered the phone.

"Hubert? Have you found the two men?" the voice asked. The voice. The raspy, older, smooth, manly voice.

A voice that Byron recognized and quickly identified. "Dr. Astronelli?" he blurted.

"Excuse me? Who is this?"

Before Byron could utter another word, he felt several sharp pains in his back. He'd been impaled by the deer antlers that had fallen from the wall minutes earlier. Loretta pushed with all her might. The pressure and the pain caused Byron's trigger finger to squeeze a shotgun bullet into Hubert's face, sending blood and flesh and brains all over the cottage.

Although the wounds weren't initially life-threatening, Byron slipped on Hubert's blood and fell backwards, his weight causing the speared antlers to tear through his flesh and puncture a few organs. He dropped the phone, blood and life quickly drained from his body. His life flashes were abrupt and nonsensical, except for the ones with Vincent—they played out slower, with significance. There had been something deep with his friend. Vincent was the only person in his life who'd given him other chances, who encouraged him to be better, who'd pulled for him to be successful and happy and to not end up like everyone else in his abusive and tortured family. All he'd wanted was to make things right and to prove to his friend he could do better, but now it seemed he would die all wrong.

"Sonny!" Loretta rushed to her son's practically headless body and then promptly vomited all over it.

"What is happening?" the doctor asked, the phone now lying on the floor two inches from Byron's outstretched, now dead hand.

Loretta crawled to the phone and put it to her ear. "It's okay. We found the guy, but he is dead. And so is my son. My son is dead. Oh my God, my poor son is dead." She started crying.

"Are you sure nobody else has escaped?"

"No."

"No, they haven't, or no, you're not sure?"

"No, they haven't escaped." Loretta calmed herself. "Please bring the money. We earned it. We deserve it. My poor, dead son deserves it."

"I hardly think money will serve your son now."

"I want the fucking money, mister!" She saw a white marble a few inches from her and grabbed it only to discover it was one of her son's eyeballs. She carried it over to his faceless head and plopped it in a cavity. It looked like a protruded, inflamed monkey asshole. With one eye. She vomited again. "I need the money for his funeral. I want an open casket!" She began crying again.

He told her to stay put and not to touch the bodies.

He was on his way to clean up the mess.

THE ANTIDOTE

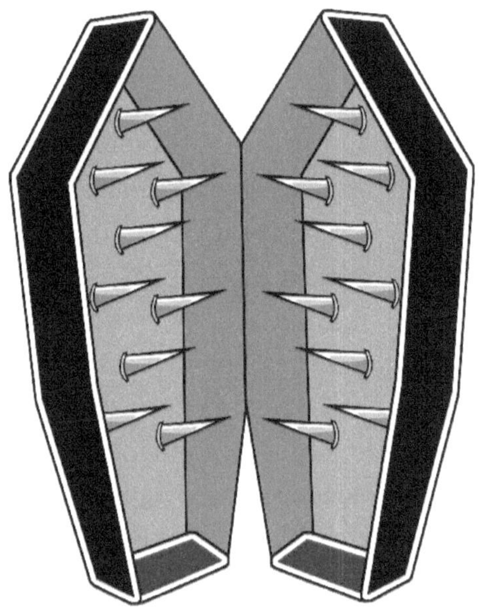

Dr. Astronelli was through with humanity. As a psychiatrist, he realized people had imperfections—sure, that was job security—but some had blemishes the size of award-winning pumpkins at a fall festival, and these pumpkins couldn't be turned into pumpkin pies. They could be dissected, cut into cubes, pureed, and cooked, but ultimately, they'd come out of the oven lumpy and devoid of flavor with crusts blacker than their souls.

Dr. Astronelli was also bipolar with sprinkles of an undiagnosed borderline personality disorder, and he had stopped taking his meds a month ago. He gradually lacked sympathy and empathy and was prone to aggression, anxiety, and psychopathic tendencies. His symptoms were stifled when he was taking his bipolar medications, as they unintentionally acted in a two-for-one manner, keeping all his disorders at bay. That didn't stop him from sketching pictures of his patients being mutilated while pretending to take notes during their therapy sessions.

Dr. Astronelli did not have a valid license to practice psychiatry. He'd lost it when he backhanded a lippy teenage boy two years earlier. This boy tried to tell him his navy-blue Ralph Lauren dress shirt didn't match his khakis and shoes, that a shirt needed to match shoes or, at the very least, socks. The doctor found this an absurd notion, and the discussion led to a physical altercation. When Astronelli defended himself to the hospital board after the boy's parents filed a complaint, they realized he wasn't entirely right in the head, which led to a revoked license while he underwent psychoanalysis. Instead of completing the assessment, he quietly fled New Jersey and hid in the quiet town of Shady Springs, Illinois, where he opened his own office and practiced medicine using his recently deceased father's medical license. His father had died at seventy. Astronelli was fifty-two and resembled his father, although his father didn't have a full, bushy, salt-and-pepper beard.

It was fitting that the younger Astronelli would take the identity of the older, as the man had spent his entire life trying to emulate his father. He constantly sought the approval and love of a man who hated him. A man who psychologically tortured his only child, using him as a guinea pig for potential new treatments and antidotes for his disturbed patients. When the younger was caught smoking marijuana as a teenager, the older tried his antidote of super-gluing a pencil between his forefinger and middle finger and then ripping them apart, layers of skin removed, leaving scars the length of the fingers. Later experiments included shock therapy for pornography habits and needles under his fingernails for eating too many sweets. After living through this torture for most of his life, the least his deceased father could do was to allow him to practice under his license.

The patient count grew steadily in Shady Springs, several being sent to the younger Astronelli by the law.

Miranda Lassort, aka *the blonde*, was one of those patients.

"He's lowlife scum," Miranda shared with Dr. Astronelli during her fifth visit to his office after being ordered by the court to seek professional therapy for psychological issues resulting in attempted murder. She had sneaked a gun into the bank where she worked and tried to shoot her boss. They were having a tumultuous affair, both married to others, and it all came to a head. He'd tried ending it with Miranda. She wasn't going quietly.

"You're the scum, Miranda. Do you know that?" the doctor asked.

"Excuse me? I'm the scum?"

"You took a gun into a federal building and tried to blow someone's head off their shoulders. This man wasn't trying to do that to you. Why is he the scum?"

"I told you many times already: he fucked me over. He loved me. He was leaving his wife. Liar!"

"What made this man more special than your husband?"

"He fucked like a jackrabbit."

"You've had intercourse with a jackrabbit?"

Miranda rolled her eyes. "Yes. Yes, I did. Yes, I do. I fuck horses too. Ever see one of their dicks? I could ride that all night long."

Astronelli opened his spiral notebook and began drawing a horse. He spent a good five minutes working on the details of the mane and ears and the twenty-four-inch penis that dragged along the dirty ground. He held up the drawing. "Like this?"

"No. Bigger. Bigger dick." Miranda stood and walked to the window. "Look, what is it I need to say or do to stop coming here? This is torture."

"How are you going to better yourself, Miranda? What changes are you going to make in your life to avoid a similar situation?"

"I'm never having sex with a married man again."

"That doesn't mean you won't get involved with a man who may lie to you."

"Der, you think, doc?"

Astronelli stood and walked to Miranda, who had turned her back to him. He grabbed her shoulder and swung her around to face him, their faces two inches apart. "Listen here, you little piece of garbage. I didn't go to college for eight years to be disrespected by filth like you. When you talk to me, you respect me, or I'll make sure you come here five days a week for a year. Do I make myself clear?"

Miranda nodded and sat back down on the sofa.

An eye blink later, Astronelli was smiling as he sat. "Now, dear, let's talk about your children. Have they been on their best behavior?"

Miranda stared at the doctor for a moment; she seemed dazed by his aggressive actions. As the doctor instructed, she discussed her children with very little emotion.

She confided to Astronelli a couple sessions later that she had contemplated reporting him but wasn't sure where to start with that process. He assured her she couldn't prove any wrongdoing, plus, she'd have to start all over with another doctor, and that was the last thing she wanted, so she continued to deal with his erratic behavior. Three months passed before he gave her a passing grade on her legal documentation but not before she succumbed to his very own horse penis. It happened once, and he called it a *test* to ensure she wouldn't go crazy and pull a gun on him once their sessions ended. She didn't pull a gun on him, but she did harass him and his sex organ. Calling at all hours and showing up unexpectedly for another dose of horse. He described her as being *dickmatized*, but she laughed that term off as something he found in the urban dictionary. She begged him for more help, but he insisted she was fine.

◎　　◎　　◎

"He'll be back, mark my words," Miranda told the others as she paced outside of camp, keeping a close eye in the direction the beast had appeared, now twice. Everyone was on edge following the visit with the mysterious man with the cyborg voice and then the creature.

"Then I kept looking because of the sound of the boastful words which the horn was speaking; I kept looking until the beast was slain, and its body was destroyed and given to the burning fire," Father Daniel preached.

"For someone who doesn't believe, you sure do know your Bible," Mia said.

It was early morning and a layer of wetness covered everything, chilling the group to the bone once again.

"I have a photographic memory. Knowing that I was going to lose my sight allowed me to prepare the files in my head. When I hear certain words or want to preach on a certain topic, I simply open that file, and I can actually see the printed words on a piece of paper. Comes in handy for Sunday sermons."

"And when you're nearing death, it seems," said Glen, barely conscious; his gunshot wound now numbing his entire body. He had no intention or strength to move if the monster came out of hiding again.

"Somewhere over there. That thing can come and go from somewhere over there." Miranda continued to pace and point toward the secret opening of the tunnel, the dark keeping her away. She had hurt her back upon landing from Rocka's blow and never recovered her spear, but she found a sewing needle.

Helen crawled from the shelter and followed Miranda. "What did he do with that lady?"

"I don't know. Screwed her? Ripped her apart and ate her?"

"Miranda, don't talk like that to the girl," Colin demanded as he sat in his tire, ass nearly touching the ground and legs in the air.

She ignored him. "All I know is he's coming back for me. If he didn't have his hands full, he would've grabbed me. I'm next. He tried to get me when I was a little girl, and he'll try to get me again."

"Come back in, Helen," Colin said. He knew Miranda was losing it and could pose a danger to the girl.

"No! I'm killing the monster."

"Okay. Good luck then."

Colin closed his eyes; the straining in the dark to see movement was exhausting. Although he felt the need to nurture someone else following the death and abduction of his first patient, he lacked the strength needed to be successful. Three tires over, Glen was panting. Mia shivered, fully awake, and Father Daniel's memory department searched for the next appropriate quote from the largest-selling book in history. Beef sat and stared, hoping to catch the scent of the trash monster, while Miranda and Helen continued to pace hand in hand.

THE DREAM

R yan was lost in a forest. He wasn't sure how he got there, but he knew of no escape. He ran through it, stumbling often but never finding an opening to a road or field or lake. He was suffocating in fall-colored leaves and thickets of fallen tree debris. Often, he felt someone or something watching him, following his every meaningless step, waiting for the right moment to snuff out his life. Thought eluded him until he encountered a large pine tree. The trunk of the tree was as wide as an above-ground swimming pool, and its branches were spread like someone's open arms awaiting a big bear hug. He pulled himself up onto the first arm and easily scaled the tree until he was a good fifty feet above the ground.

"Help me!"

The tops of the trees surrounding him swayed, the winds more forceful at that height. He thought he would see something that high, a clearing or structure to direct him out of the woods, but all he saw were more trees and leaves.

"Help me!"

This time, those words didn't come from his mouth but from the mouth of a woman. They flowed with the wind to his ears. He scanned the trees but couldn't see down very far. A shine caught his right peripheral, and he turned to find a beautiful woman swinging in the tree next to him. Somehow there was a swing, like the ones you chain to a tree branch in your backyard. She swung back and forth, flying high above the other trees, her long brown hair blowing.

"Help me!"

This swinging beauty was not the one yelling for help. Ryan looked to his left, and another woman appeared. She was also swinging but differently than the other: she was swaying from a noose around her neck. She was purple, dead for quite a while it seemed. He shuddered and squeezed his eyes shut, hoping this vision would be gone when he opened them again.

"Help me!"

It came from the branch below him this time. Another beautiful, model-like African American woman grabbed his foot and pulled him from his perch. He fell backward, unable to latch onto another branch. He fell five stories, hitting every branch on his way to the hard ground. He landed with a thud and was sure that he was dead. He opened his eyes to find the woman who'd made him fall lowering herself onto him like a spider, webbing exiting her anus. She started kissing him and undressing him with the four arms and hands she possessed.

"Help me!"

Ryan gasped and awoke in his bed, his sheets wet with sweat. It was five in the morning, and he had just fallen asleep an hour ago. He hated sleeping alone. He felt vulnerable. Fully awake now, he slid from his puddled bed and stumbled to the bathroom.

His work starting time was eight, and he typically checked in at the office before going out in the field, but he decided since he was up, he would visit the old Carlyle Dump first and then check in to the office. Besides, it would give him some brownie points with Jamal, who always seemed to be pissed at him about something.

The hot shower washed away the weird dream and the thoughts of the bird with the broken neck. Ryan didn't like weirdness. He functioned best with monotony. Rebecca leaving triggered many ADHD symptoms, including anxiety and absentmindedness. The latter symptom caused him to forget his mobile phone as he began his journey from Chicago to Shady Springs. He programmed his dashboard GPS unit to direct him to Gladstone Park, the park closest to the old dump. He would stop there first to check the streams; his contamination test kits in the back seat of his Jeep Cherokee Sport.

Fifteen miles into the trip, Ryan thought about his phone and patted the front, right pocket of his trousers, discovering nothing but fabric. He panicked and pulled off the freeway. He sat for twelve minutes, trying to decide if he should go back. He finally chose to continue toward the park; the retreat would take too much time. The sun began its ascent as he passed the gravel drive that led to the old Carlyle Dump. Two miles later, he parked at a shelter house and jumped out of his Jeep. He grabbed a light jacket and threw it on, the early chill a bit much.

After a small climb down an embankment, he arrived at the stream. He searched for life in the knee-deep water and saw nothing. Not a fish or a frog or a snake. He removed his kit, placed his test tubes in their designated positions on the stand, and gathered water samples that needed to be taken to a lab. Results usually took twenty-four to forty-eight hours.

He thought about Rebecca not being at home when he returned after a long day of work. It hurt him more than he imagined it would in the scenario played in his head previously when he'd considered breaking up with her. He wanted to text her a hello and ask how she was but quickly remembered he had no phone. The trickling water of the stream helped him remember a trip they took to a resort in the wild of Pennsylvania a couple years ago. They hiked to a secluded waterfall and engaged in a little skinny-dipping. It had taken a bit of persuading for Rebecca to lose her clothing, but when she finally did and stood under the falls, it was a truly magical moment.

And it only lasted a moment.

A family of beavers fell onto their heads from the top of the falls, scratching and knocking them under the water. Rebecca nearly lost her left nipple. She was furious with Ryan for talking her into going nude.

Shaking his head, Ryan chuckled at the memory as he finished the water collection, packed everything back into the case, and made his way back up the hill. He was a few feet from the top when he slipped on the wet grass. He and the case of water samples rolled down the slope and plunged into the cold water. Ryan screamed and scrambled to his feet as a current grabbed the case. By the time he realized it had been stolen, it was nearly out of sight, turning the corner ahead. And then it was gone.

"Why? Why?" Ryan shouted, realizing there wasn't a way of saving the case, not in his drenched state and with the speed of the current.

He crawled out of the water and lay back against the muddy base of the hill. This was it for him. If he went to the office with a missing case and no water samples, Jamal would surely hand him his walking papers. Hell, it'd be more like his walking, self-sticking notepad, since he hadn't been there long enough to warrant a full sheet of paper.

Then he remembered that the soil sample kit was still in his Jeep. Once he returned the soil samples to the lab, he could check in to the office as usual, not mention losing the water kit, grab a new one, and head back out, which was Jamal's original plan for him, anyway. He took a deep breath and smiled. He still had a chance. It was all going to be fine, he thought as he continued up the hill and to his Jeep.

A mile away from the gravel path to the old Carlyle Dump, his Jeep laughed at his thought of being fine and promptly ran out of gas.

◎   ◎   ◎

"I still don't have my money."

Back at the bloody cottage on the hill, Loretta wanted her cash. Dr. Astronelli ignored her as he collected the last little pile of Hubert from the corner of the room.

"My son lost his life for this money. We did everything you asked us to do. I memorized all the stories and things to say to each of them people. We got them all here in the hole. We—"

"If you got them all in the hole, Loretta, I wouldn't be cleaning your son's brains off the floor, would I?"

"Oh, Hubert." She covered her mouth with her hands, looking sad for about two seconds. "So, do you have the money? Will it be larger bills, or do you have a mixture? Smaller bills work better for my buys at the dollar store. Larger would be better for stuff around the house. I had my eye on a new vacuum."

Astronelli tied the bag of Hubert's head remains and walked around the corner to the bathroom to wash his hands. Something caught his eye as he passed Hubert's bedroom, and he stopped for a look. The fluorescent-orange, thirteen-gallon trash bags he had instructed them to throw in the landfill after all the victims were placed were still in the cottage. This was a critical part of the plan left unfinished. He walked back to the blood-soaked living room and grabbed Loretta by the throat.

"You stupid old hag! You and your dumb-as-rocks son screwed everything up. And you want paid? You're lucky I don't kill you!" He pushed her back on the sofa. She coughed. "You can see this isn't my fault. My plan was solid from the onslaught. Good help is impossible to find," he said, not really directing it to Loretta.

Ten minutes later, the bags and Loretta were loaded into his vehicle.

◉   ◉   ◉

Ryan arrived at the bottom of the gravel path after jogging a mile from his dead vehicle. His plan was to gather the soil and then flag down a car to get him to a gas station. He could still pull off getting to the office on time if every single step that followed happened without a snag. As he worked his way up the path, he had no clue that the landfill was so far back, as it was taking him forever to arrive. This was a snag he was hoping to avoid.

And then he came upon the cottage: huge snag number two. Unbeknown to him, the doctor and granny had just left.

The door swung open and almost closed and then completely opened and completely closed, except it wasn't latching.

"Hello?" Ryan called, about ten steps away. After a minute of no response, he looked around the area and saw nothing but woods and the gravel path continuing up a slight incline and curving out of sight behind a cluster of trees. He proceeded to the cottage to investigate, knowing this wasn't the best idea for his tight time restraint.

"Hello?" He was at the door, which was currently closed. When he reached for the handle, it blew completely open and stayed open, the rising sun illuminating the filthy, blood-stained living room. "Holy shit."

He stepped inside, and the door slammed closed, this time latching. He quickly turned and grabbed the handle, thinking he needed to leave immediately, but morbid curiosity got the best of him, forcing him to spin around and inspect. He shivered, still soaked from his fall earlier as well as creeped out by the amount of red that colored the sofa and floor and walls. He wished to God it was a paint spill, but he knew better. The omen of the dead bird entered his brain. Maybe it wasn't a sign his relationship would die. Perhaps he would encounter the literal death of a human person. Goosebumps popped from his arms.

"Is anyone here?" he asked, not wanting an answer, as he realized if someone was there, he would be the next to spill red in the room.

He shivered as a sense of dread overtook him.

THE BAGS

Miranda and Helen and Beef were curled together just outside the base camp when the morning light raised its head. They were so exhausted they didn't wake up. Colin was the first one to rise and stretch and survey the surroundings, as if anything would change after twelve hours of darkness. Besides a missing dead woman, of course. He was amazed he was mostly injury-free. Minor cuts and scrapes only. Helen had a deep cut on her left arm, but it seemed to be clean and safe. The only one with a major injury was Glen and his shot-gunned arm. He needed medical attention soon or risked losing his arm and possibly his life if the infection grew.

Colin was still confident they were escaping today. Everyone had seen the beast, and it was true what Miranda suggested: that it was getting in and out somehow. Finding its escape route and avoiding getting killed were the tasks of day three of consciousness. Hunger was forgotten, as their minds focused on reconnecting with their lives outside of the dump.

And then an alarm sounded.

A car horn from above awakened everyone. They tried to focus on the source, but no part of the vehicle was spotted.

A stuffed, orange trash bag took flight, landing a few yards from camp. Helen raced after it.

"What is happening?" Father Daniel asked and was ignored for the thirty-second time.

"Stop!" Colin yelled at Helen as she climbed into the trash. She ignored him. "Helen, stop!" She complied this time, turning to him. "We don't know what's in there. This is a game. Please be careful."

She continued to the orange bag and grabbed it. She shook it lightly and then scrambled to exit the filth, holding the bag above her head. She dropped it in front of the others, and Colin untied the knot and spread the opening. It was stuffed with crumpled newspapers, but once those were removed, he uncovered envelopes with each of their names typed on the fronts. He passed them out, all except for Byron, Punam, and Carl, of course.

"Stop!" It was the cyborg voice again.

They refrained from opening their envelopes and looked up at the figure in the long black trench coat with a newsboy cap and sunglasses holding a megaphone. It was the shadow from last night, now visible but no more recognizable. Another figure stepped forward, holding a shotgun. This one was completely recognizable.

Mia pointed. "It's her, oh my God!"

"You bitch!" Miranda threw a large rock, not even close to leaving the hole. Loretta squeezed the trigger and shot a tire a foot from the group.

"Read. Go first, Mia," Cyborg Astronelli instructed.

Mia opened her small envelope and unfolded a piece of paper. The font was small, and it didn't fill up much of the page. She started reading to herself.

"Read aloud! No pre-reading permitted!" screamed the figure.

"What is happening, Mr. Roboto?" Daniel asked.

"My name is Mia, and I'm a backstabbing, fame-seeking whore." She looked up at the man, who instructed her to keep reading. "I slept with the head of a talent agency to get my role on the hit show *Aces of Slade*." Her voice faded.

"Speak up! I want to hear. If your voice dips again, Grandma is blowing your head off."

"Okay!" She continued, "And even then, I was not their first choice. My roommate was, and I talked her out of taking the role, scaring her from it by lying about being fondled by the director. The role was then offered to me, and I graciously accepted. I slept with several of the directors throughout the first season when I heard rumors they were going to recast me. I am a talentless fake. I had a nose and boob job. I acknowledge I am a bad human being and ask for help." She folded the letter and put it back in the envelope. "These are lies, all lies."

"All true. Everything you will hear is true," Dr. Cyborg said. "Read your letters to the others without incident, and you will be rewarded." Astronelli handed the megaphone to Loretta. "Make sure they all read. I'll be back."

"Are you gonna pay me?"

"Yes." The joy of the moment was lost as he realized he needed more weapons and ammunition. Besides, he really didn't need to hear the pathetic confessions. He jumped in his car and sped away.

They took turns doing as instructed, reading their admissions of crime and wrongdoings aloud, checking from time to time to see if the shotgun was still pointing at them. This experimental group therapy session helped them to realize that their connection was a questionable therapist named Dr. Astronelli.

"I knew it! Disgusting!" Miranda told Glen after his letter detailed his womanizing and pedophilia past. "You should be in prison, you pig."

Glen became lightheaded and sat down, unable to argue or process his controversial past being exposed.

His career would certainly be over if they made it out alive.

Colin read Father Daniel's letter, and it covered most of what he had already shared with them. He sought help to become a better person, hoping it would make him a better priest.

Colin's letter differed completely from the others. It seemed his only crime was being gay, as he had been the victim of a hate crime and suffered from depression and thoughts of suicide. He was being punished by the one person who was supposed to help him. He recalled the session when the bandage was ripped from the wound.

◉   ◉   ◉

"Do you have sexual intercourse with your male friends?" Astronelli asked Colin out of the blue, causing a slight case of flabbergast.

"No, I don't." This therapy session had taken place a year ago, and Colin had been with Jack for a year. "But I am in a committed relationship, so it's not like I have more than one guy that I have sex with right now."

The doctor interrogated Colin on his sexual practices and the extent of sexual partners at one time. Colin confessed to being with two guys at once, and Astronelli needed detailed accounts of what had happened sexually in that tryst. Colin balked.

"I'm asking a very important question, Colin. I need to understand your sexual needs and the sexual requirements within your community. In the heterosexual world, there aren't as many sexual options." Colin wasn't sure if he legitimately needed to understand the ins and outs of gay sex to better help him, or if there was a more personal interest. He shared the gritty details, resulting in expressions of alarm and discomfort from the doctor followed by an awkward silence.

Colin searched for the right words to explain an incident that had occurred in his sophomore year of college. He'd been at a fraternity party with a good friend who was looking to pledge in the fraternity. He had a girlfriend, but she had to study for an exam and decided to skip the party. Colin had messed around with a buddy in high school but never identified with the homosexual community. He felt he didn't fit the stereotype; therefore, he wasn't gay. His attractions and desires for men came and went, and he had them under control.

And then he met Andy at the frat party.

Andy was a jock, a quarterback on the college football team, a beautiful man he'd admired a few times from afar. He bumped into him at the party, and they started chatting. Chatting led to his bedroom where they smoked some pot, picked up each other's signals, and ended up naked in Andy's bed. At a certain point in their play, Andy rolled Colin onto his stomach and penetrated him, the immediate pain causing Colin to shove him off. And then a frat brother barged through the bedroom door and stepped into the dark room. Andy quickly pushed Colin under the covers.

"I wondered where you were hiding, bro." The brother stepped toward the bed, clearly drunk. Andy shook his head and pointed to the lump under his comforter. "Oh, I see." He chuckled and stepped backward, running into three other brothers entering the room.

"Man, what are you doing in bed?"

Andy spouted a quickly conceived lie. "I have a female friend under here. Can you guys give me minute? I'll be right out."

"Who is she?"

"Nobody. C'mon, she'll be embarrassed. Give us some space."

"Okay." They started to leave but then turned back to the bed and ripped the comforter off, exposing Colin.

"Holy shit!" Andy said. "What the fuck are you doing?" He kicked naked Colin to the floor. "Guys, I don't know what's going on here. I was passed out, and someone crawled under my covers. I thought it was a chick." He kicked Colin again before putting on jeans. "Get the fuck out of here, faggot!"

The other brothers also started in on Colin, all too drunk to realize the story was ridiculous. They started kicking Colin as well, preventing him from putting his clothing back on. They ended up pushing him out naked into the center of the party crowd while telling everyone he'd molested Andy. He eventually fled, his friend giving him his jacket to cover his nakedness. The friend never got into the fraternity, and Colin dropped out of that college shortly after the incident, nobody believing his side of the story, not even his friend.

"Wow. That is a traumatic incident. Life-altering, in fact," Astronelli said, "and, therefore, you don't allow a man to get on you because of the trauma of that incident?"

Colin chuckled at his terminology. "I imagine so, yes. Plus, I couldn't walk for a couple days after that, and it wasn't from the kicks to my ribs."

"Now I understand, Colin."

Their therapy sessions continued, and Colin found himself more comfortable and open about sharing the physical and emotional aspects of being attracted to men. It was very instrumental in helping Colin overcome his own homophobia.

But now this man was using all of this information against him.

◎　　◎　　◎

A vehicle pulled up outside the cottage, trapping Ryan inside as he discreetly glanced out the window and saw a man with a hat and large black sunglasses stepping out of the car and quickly approaching the broken front door.

Ryan's goosebumps extended to every pore on his body as he urgently scanned the room for a hiding spot, settling for the coat closet facing the front door. He barely pulled the door closed when the front door flew open and the man in black entered the cottage of blood. He held his breath as the man passed outside the closet door. The door was made of slanted wood slats that allowed some vision through them, and the closet was small enough that Ryan's body was up against the door. He saw the man's pants and shoes and heard a clatter in the room with the blood. Clatter led to glass shattering, and a conversation ensued. The two different voices were distinct, but it was obvious they were coming from the same man.

"I know. I heard you the first time."

"Why haven't you done it then?"

"I'm heading out now, Father."

"Do it, and discontinue the insolence, or I'll give you something to really whimper about. There's a special chair for you in the cellar."

"Yeah. Hey, Dad—oops, I meant *Father*. Sorry, I know *Dad* is a little too feely for you. How are you feeling today? Not well? Aw, so sorry to hear that. Here, I brought you some of your favorite whiskey. Have a swig. You like? Guess what, *Dad*? It wasn't your favorite whiskey after all. It was the toilet water from my bowel movement this morning." Astronelli started laughing, and Ryan heard him loading bullets into a gun.

"I told your mother to abort you."

"Was I really that big of a disappointment to you? You haven't spoken to me in years, Father, and you only live ten miles from me."

"You destroyed everything your grubby little hands encountered."

"Yeah, you're correct. I was a troubled individual. Every boy deserves to be tortured for touching themselves. Or for reading Shakespeare. Perfectly acceptable causes for punishment."

The man threw something else against the wall, providing another explosion of glass. Ryan wasn't sure he'd survive a fight with this deeply troubled character. He prayed the closet door stayed closed.

"Tough man. Acting out doesn't make you strong; it makes you inadequate and pathetic."

"How are you feeling about me now, Father?"

"What did you do?"

"Oh, don't try to get up; it will be unsightly to see you fall on your face. Besides, I want you to look into my eyes until the very last second. Why are you grabbing your chest? Pain? Yeah, Father. That's right. Cardiac arrest."

"Didn't even have the guts to fight me like a man. You're weak."

"Maybe, but I'm not dying today. And while I'd love to kick you a few hundred times after you fall, this is supposed to look like a death from natural causes, so pass on over to whatever place called hell you're headed toward, Father. But do me a favor and stay away from Mommy."

Astronelli knocked over a large piece of furniture, more glass and miscellaneous trinkets shattering everywhere.

Ryan felt like *he* was going into cardiac arrest. His heart was beating so fast and seemingly loud that he was sure this man would hear it and kill him like he apparently did his father. But based on the conversation, he couldn't have murdered his father here. There was too much blood. He tried to take shallow breaths as he imagined explaining this to Jamal. This would be a legitimate excuse for not making it to the landfill again and for being late.

"How was I cursed with a shit heel for a son?"

It was continuing. Hadn't the old man in the story died yet?

"Yeah, okay, I'm a turd, but at least I've created an astonishing experiment. Something you wouldn't have come up with if you were alive another twenty years."

"You fucked it up. Excuse my French."

"No, I didn't. These idiots did. You can't count on anyone but yourself these days. Have you even witnessed what I've done? I've gathered an impressive group of unstable people, ones who wouldn't heal by conventional therapy."

"Once a shit heel, always a shit heel."

"You would be so proud of me, Father, finally."

Ryan sensed the shift in the discussion from the father's pre-murder voice to the deceased father's voice.

The man laughed maniacally and started for the front door, his pointed dress shoes and legs coming into Ryan's view through the door once again. The man paused at the open front door and turned to the closet door. One step would get him to the door, and one tug on the doorknob would expose Ryan. One kick to

Ryan's face would kill him, but why would he need to kick when he possessed a gun?

Ryan farted. He lost control, his stomach a hot mess. He squeezed his eyes shut and held his breath, waiting for the door to fly open.

The man screamed at the top of his lungs. Then he kicked the closet door, his foot breaking a couple slats of wood, which rammed into Ryan's head, knocking him back as part of the closet door separated slightly but didn't fall apart. It still hid Ryan's now unconscious body.

"I am not a shit heel!"

Dr. Astronelli left the cottage, oblivious to the man in the closet. He drove back to the landfill, the quarter-mile path allowing his anger to increase. Now it was focused on Hubert and Loretta and on how they had destroyed his plan to properly rehabilitate his former patients below. He was coming up to Loretta, five feet from the edge of the landfill, singing into the megaphone. He pushed down on the gas pedal and came up to her quickly. She had no time to react.

He plowed into her and sent her flying, slamming on the brakes and spinning in time to stop inches from the edge of the landfill. He watched her fly over the makeshift campground. The captives quickly scattered below as she landed on double-stacked tires, bounced back into the air, flipped a couple times, and slammed into the other side of the wall. She slid down the wall like a character in a *Looney Tunes* cartoon, and her body collapsed onto itself like a slinky.

The group stared at her and then up at the vehicle as the doctor stepped out, without his disguise. He had planned on revealing his identity later in the game but given the incompetence of the execution of his plan he figured now was as good as later. Fortunately, Loretta dropped the megaphone at the landing. *She actually did something right before her death*, Astronelli thought as he retrieved it.

He retired the cyborg voice and spoke normally into the bullhorn, "Hello. Are you all done confessing your dirty little secrets to each other? How does it feel to be standing next to someone just as revolting as yourself? Is there a sense of competition, perhaps?" He laughed. "I bet you wish you had been a little more serious about your recovery when you were in my office. No worries, my friends. Hope remains for each of you. I'm here to fix you again, since I failed the first time around. But first, how about some refreshments?"

He grabbed another orange bag from his back seat and launched it into the hole. This one landed with a thud, a little harder than the first bag. Astronelli's original plan had called for the bags to already be hidden among the trash. A bit more of a challenge to retrieve them.

Colin drudged through the trash to retrieve the bag and returned to the others with nine bottled waters and nine individually wrapped pastries that looked like brownies.

One of the brownies was laced with cyanide.

THE BROWNIE

Glen Hampton wasn't always so sexually charged. He hadn't lost his virginity until the age of twenty-one, much later than his high school and college buddies, although he told them his cherry had popped at age thirteen.

The very first time he had sex, he impregnated the girl. This girl became his wife, as she didn't believe in abortion, and both sets of parents had forced them to marry. The first year or two of marriage was good—a journey he'd always known he would take, just not so soon and not with a girl he barely knew. Getting to know each other in such an extreme manner seemed to work at first, but the tribulations of parenting drove a wedge between them.

Glen was not a good father.

His days were spent working at the convenience store on the corner of their Chicago street, and his nights were spent taking college courses. The little time he was available to spend with his son, he was tired and highly irritable.

Four years into the marriage, he had his first affair. He was interning at a local radio station where he met Tina, the station manager, ten years older. She taught him much about sex—something his wife could not do. His wife didn't even like sex. The affairs continued over the years, and his wife was suspicious from time to time, but Glen always fibbed his way out. He was an amazing deceiver.

"Hi, Dad," Glen's son, Colton, said as he tossed his schoolbooks on the kitchen table. He was in the ninth grade and the ripe, young age of fifteen.

"Hi, Colton. Good day at the office?" Glen joked before a striking, blond-haired, blue-eyed beauty walked in the house, following Colton. "Hello there."

"Hi."

"Who's your friend, son?" he asked Colton, not realizing he had left the room. He heard him in the half bathroom down the hall doing his business.

"I'm Christina."

"Christina? Pretty name. I knew a Tina once." He smiled at her, deciding that was an uncool thing to say.

He couldn't look away, his eyes scanning her slender body and her perky breasts, which were slightly exposed on the outside of the snug, V-neck blouse. She was not naïve; Glen knew full well that she appreciated the attention. She appeared a little older than his son, but with girls these days, it was sometimes hard to decipher ages.

After an awkward silence and a couple looks away from each other, the girl spoke, "What's your name?"

"I'm Glen. Do you recognize me?" He had recently celebrated his one-year anniversary with the Chicago television station WLBV.

"No. Should I?"

Glen chuckled. The line didn't really work just yet, for he hadn't been on the air that much. "I'm a meteorologist. I report the weather on the boob tube." He looked at her boobs and felt his face flush, not intending to use those exact words.

"Sounds fun." Christina leaned forward, resting her elbows on the back of the kitchen chair, as if accepting an unspoken invitation to show her boob tubes. "You probably talk a lot about the winds and which directions they blow." She made intimate eye contact with Glen when she said *blow*, and his dick turned to steel. She smiled and looked down at his crotch. He quickly put his hands in his pockets and adjusted himself.

"Dad!"

Glen panicked, thinking his son knew of his erection. "What?"

Colton walked past him to the kitchen sink. "The sink is still broken in the bathroom."

Glen exhaled and regained his composure. "Sorry. I'll work on it later."

Colton washed his hands and grabbed a towel. "I see you met my girlfriend."

"Yes. Oh, wait, your girlfriend?"

"Yes," Colton said confidently as Christina rolled her eyes and turned her head away from him.

"How long have the two of you been dat—er, seeing…? What do they call it nowadays?"

Christina licked her lips. "Fucking."

"Um, what?" Glen nervously chuckled while adjusting his hard penis again.

"Funning. Having fun, no real label," she said.

"Really? I thought we were boyfriend and girlfriend," said Glen's confused son.

"I'm a girl. And your friend. Call it what you like. Now, how about that math help?"

Colton paused to process her statement and then reached for his books. "Shit."

"Language, son," Glen said, his eyes reconnecting with the young breasts that were within reach.

"Sorry, but I forgot my math book at school. C'mon, let's go get it." He grabbed Christina's arm, and she pulled it away from him.

"I'll wait here."

"Okay. I'll run. It won't take that long." Colton rushed out the door, leaving behind a very horny teenage girl and a man who shouldn't be left alone with a very horny teenage girl.

"Where's Mrs. Hampton?"

"Work."

"I work too."

"You do? Where is that?"

"My dad's shoe store. I stock the shoes and sweep the sock lint off the carpet."

"Sock lint, huh?"

"You wouldn't believe how much furry stuff sticks to my carpet." Christina stepped closer to Glen, her left hand sensually gliding down the side of her body.

◎　　◎　　◎

"What did you do then, Glen?" Dr. Astronelli asked. It was their third session, and this was the first time he'd brought up his illegal attractions.

Glen stood and paced the room. "I bent her over the kitchen table. Oh my God, I can't believe I just verbalized that. I never set out to have sex with an underage girl. I—"

"Statutory rape is what it's called. Not sex."

"Please don't say that."

"It's true."

"But she asked for it. She seduced me."

"She's a girl."

"A mature girl."

"What happened next?"

"She agreed to allow my son to call her his girlfriend, even though he had no clue what that entailed. Fortunately, he wasn't ready for sex. But she was at the house a lot, and we had sex a couple more times, until her mother suspected she was no longer a virgin, got into her e-mail, found one from me, and then the whole thing exploded. Quietly, though."

"Quietly?"

"Turns out her mother was Tina, the station manager I had an affair with years ago. She was afraid our affair would come out and her marriage destroyed, so she agreed to keep quiet about Christina if I stopped screwing her and if Christina broke up with Colton and had nothing to do with either of us. So, she dumped my son, and I never saw her again."

"Your son never found out you were having intercourse with his girlfriend?"

"No. But it really wasn't a major deal. He never had sex with her. Honestly, I'm not sure he's lost his virginity. He doesn't seem to care about sex. He got that from his mother."

"Did you see any other underage girls after that experience?"

Glen repositioned himself on the sofa and cleared his throat. "Is our time up yet for today?"

"Is that a *yes* answer?"

"I'm sorry, Doc. There's just something so tantalizing about them."

"You need to stop. You need to stop now."

He didn't stop and continued to share the stories with Astronelli, who clearly became more and more frustrated with him. The doctor determined that since Glen had never been with a girl when he was younger, he'd missed out on his sexual awakening, and on a subconscious level, he was behaving in that manner as an adult. It was like he was in high school again, as his son brought over various girlfriends, and with more exposure on the evening news, Glen became recognizable and reached a celebrity status that he used to seduce the girls and other women. He eventually stopped seeing Astronelli, arrogantly deciding his actions were fine.

◎   ◎   ◎

But Dr. Astronelli didn't stop seeing Glen. He watched him every night on the news and was constantly reminded of his failure to cure the weatherman of his sickness. He heard his father relentlessly berating him for his failure.

"Has the weatherman touched you inappropriately, Helen?" the doctor asked through his bullhorn from the ledge above.

Helen looked at Glen and then up to her former psychiatrist. "No."

"She's just a girl, for crying out loud!"

"She's only a couple years younger than some of your conquests, Glen. Why stop at fifteen?" Astronelli snickered, thrilled at the power he had over these deficient people. "I'm sure he didn't tell you about Christy. Did he tell you where he met this girl? At a high school volleyball game. He claimed to be there for a news story. A weather story at an indoor volleyball game. How wonderfully compelling. But nobody questioned. Why would they? People love him. And he's remarkably good-looking. That helps."

"Please stop."

"He preys on the single mothers first. And then he seduces their daughters."

"Shut the fuck up!" Glen yelled, but it didn't travel far. It seemed his weakened state was preventing him from projecting. "I begged them for forgiveness when you left. Why rehash anything more?"

"Why would you beg them for forgiveness? They have no bearing on your atrocities. It is me you need to beg. It was my time you squandered."

Colin began passing out the water, unable to wait for the cat-and-mouse dialogue to end. The bottles were frantically opened, and everyone started guzzling. It was as if they were all at a college party, taking part in a beer-chugging contest.

"Stop!" Colin said. "Slow down. Don't drink it all. Save at least half."

Mia started gagging and projectile vomited her water, having drank so quickly. Beef slurped it off the ground. Helen cupped her hand and allowed Beef to drink some of her water as well.

"What else is in that bag?" Miranda snagged the orange trash bag from next to Colin and reached in, pulling out a handful of the individually wrapped squares, each the size of a Zippo lighter. She held them to her nose. "Brownies?" She passed them out, holding the three extra in her hand. They started unwrapping.

Astronelli watched. And smiled. He felt like a shark circling his victims.

"Stop!" Colin said again. "We can't trust this guy. We can't just pop anything he gives us in our mouths." He peered up at Astronelli, who was thrilled at what was about to happen. "Why are you giving us food and water? Why feed us if you just want to kill us?"

"Who said I wanted you dead?"

"C'mon, it's food!" Miranda pleaded, salivating.

"But we drank the water, and it didn't hurt us," Helen said.

"Those delicious brownies are an old family recipe. From my grandmother. There are nuts in them, though, so if you have nut allergies, beware. Although, we know that won't affect you, Colin, given your love of nuts." The doctor cackled through the horn.

"How do we know they're not poisoned?" Colin screamed up.

"You don't know that I guess. Eat at your own risk."

"Smell like a normal brownie to you, Father?" Colin handed the priest an unwrapped piece.

Father Daniel inhaled deeply, trying to confirm it was indeed a brownie. "Smells like chocolate-covered rot to me."

"There wasn't a baked good my grandmother couldn't master. Her Battenberg cake was the stuff of legends; the checkered pink-and-yellow sponge cake simply melted in your mouth. And the apricot-jammed center and marzipan icing made it simply delightful."

Colin looked at Beef. "We need a guinea pig. Or a dog."

Helen hugged Beef. "No!"

"Look, he's a great dog, and if the brownies are poisonous, he should know. He wouldn't eat something with poison, right? Besides, would you rather one of us die?" Colin tried to reason with the girl.

"Yes." She pointed to Glen, and everyone except for the blind priest nodded in approval. Glen should die before the dog.

"What? Why? Because I love? Is that a fucking crime? At least I didn't try to commit murder like you!" He pointed to Miranda. "You're the psycho down here. Besides the one standing up there, I mean." He lifted his good arm toward the doctor above.

"Speak up down there, especially if you're talking about me. Don't you know it's rude to talk behind someone's back?"

Miranda opened a brownie and shoved it in her mouth. She chewed three times and swallowed. "That was fucking fantastic! Firm, yet moist. Chocolate with a hint of nuts. Asshole's grandmother really was a good cook."

Everyone quickly unwrapped their chocolate squares, unable to wait any longer.

"Stop!" Colin said once again. "If it was poisoned, she wouldn't drop dead immediately. Let's wait a moment."

It was too late for Father Daniel who had just swallowed his without chewing. "Oops."

"And now we have two guinea pigs."

They paused and stared at Miranda and Daniel, looking for a reaction or waiting for them to fall over dead.

Astronelli hummed the theme song to *Jeopardy*, the infamous melody bouncing around in the filth hole. He also spun around the edge above, dancing with himself.

"Shut up!" Mia screamed. "I can't take this." She popped a brownie in her mouth and immediately moaned—not because she had eaten the poisoned one, but because her mouth was exploding with flavor and delight. The rest of them followed, each of them savoring the small, tasty nugget. Glen started crying. He enjoyed it so much. But nobody dropped to the ground in pain.

"I told you they are delicious. Don't let the remaining three go to waste." The doctor watched in suspense. He had viewed a couple seasons of that *Survivor* show and relished the eliminations at the end of each episode.

"Here, Beef." Helen unwrapped one of the three and fed it to the German shepherd. He swallowed it whole. "I know, right? Hungry boy." Helen kissed him on the snout.

"And then there were two."

Colin held the remaining wrapped brownies in his hand as they all looked at them. Which of the starving would get a second?

Astronelli put his hand in his pocket, brushing it against the cold metal from the barrel of one of the weapons he had swiped from Hubert's gun cabinet. If something went awry with the poison, he had a backup plan.

Someone had to die.

"Give them to the women," Glen uttered. They all looked at him, shocked at the selfless gesture. "What? I'm not a bad man, I tell you. I am not a child molester, okay?"

"Okay, but you're married," Mia pointed out.

"Seriously, kettle? Do you really want to judge?"

"Look, if it's down to the women, let those two have them. They need them more than me." Mia motioned to Miranda and Helen, and Colin graciously plopped a brownie in each of their outstretched hands.

They began to unwrap.

Astronelli giggled, the bullhorn by his side, as he didn't want to give a warning. He didn't want to spoil the outcome.

Miranda was the first to unwrap, and she popped it in her mouth and chewed.

Glen screamed and fell to his side. "My fucking arm."

Colin pulled the cloth away and inspected the wound. It was infected and smelled terrible. He almost gagged. Astronelli was annoyed at the distraction. Glen needed to be the center of attention. He always needed to be the one to say something witty or inspiring at the end of each newscast, talking over the other personalities.

Helen finally completed her brownie unwrapping, and as she raised it to her mouth, her buddy, police dog Chad, now known as Beef, jumped at it, having distinguished the scent of poison, and snatched it in his mouth. He did not intend to eat it but to grab it with his teeth and then spit it out, but the speed of the jump caused the brownie to fly down the back of his throat, forcing him to swallow it.

"Beef! If you wanted it that bad, I would've given it to you," Helen said. Beef walked back to Helen and rubbed against her leg as if to apologize. She sat, and the dog curled up on her lap, wise enough to know what he swallowed was going to hurt him.

"Have all the brownies been eaten?" Astronelli asked, the commotion with Glen and the dog confusing him what had happened. And then the dog began to squeal in pain, the high pitch easily making it up to the doctor.

"Beef? Beef! What's wrong?"

It became clear to Astronelli that the dog had been the one voted out of the landfill. And this was completely unacceptable. "So, my lovely patients, I did, in fact, poison one of the brownies, as you can see from the pain and imminent death of the canine. Unfortunately, I never counseled the dog."

Helen squeezed the dog against her chest and began to cry. "No, Beef, you can't die. You have to save us. Please, don't die, please!" She buried her face in his fur, and the animal began to convulse and vomit. Colin pulled her away. "No! I want to be with him!"

"You can't. You don't want the poison on you." Colin held Helen back as they watched Beef vomit and fall to the ground.

"You son of a bitch!" Miranda screamed to Astronelli, who was enjoying the show before he proceeded with the next scene. It seemed the poisoning of the beloved dog had turned out to be the most effectual death within the group. It certainly made for quality entertainment.

◙　　◙　　◙

Beef's death was quick, less than a minute, and although painful, it wasn't nearly as extreme as the pain he'd suffered at the hands of the old man and old woman who kept him captive in that tiny metal enclosure they called his home. The infrequent feedings and name calling were more painful than death. But after a minute, he appeared at a bridge and witnessed an intensity of vivid colors—colors he could not see on Earth. On the other end of the wooden bridge stood the figure of someone he knew and loved, and he raced across that bridge so quickly it was as if he were flying. He jumped into the arms of his partner, Officer Greenwell.

"Chad, buddy! I've missed you!" Greenwell was licked profusely, although Beef's tongue was non-existent, and the dog really wasn't in his arms. They were both suspended in the air, weightless.

"How about we take that trip to Oz?"

THE CHIME

Father Daniel awoke every morning at precisely six, not because his body was on a natural schedule but because the church bell rang. He hated that bell at six in the morning. He warmed up to the noon chime, and by the time the final chime of the day sounded at six in the evening, he embraced it, using the indicator to make peace with his life. He recited the Lord's Prayer and then asked for guidance from above. The *from above* could've been the clouds or the big oak tree outside his window for all he knew. He asked open-ended questions but never received replies. He was hopeful an answer would come one day, but he wasn't holding his breath in anticipation. "I feel like there's a little person sitting on my shoulder all the time who I engage in conversation with because I'm always talking to myself," Father Daniel told his therapist, Dr. Astronelli.

His sister suggested he talk with someone about his holy issues. She was an atheist and was tired of him whining to her about it all. But the topic of faith turned into confessions of sexual activities in the confessional and regrets about life decisions. The doctor told Daniel he very much enjoyed their sessions, but long minutes passed without a peep from him, leading the blind, supposed man of God to gather he was napping.

"Your words are empty, and people will discover this," he told Daniel on their very last session.

"How will they discover?"

"You talk to yourself all the time. You don't think the nuns hear these things?"

"They're not around."

"How do you know? You can't see."

"Good point."

"I strongly believed in my priest when I was a child. I needed to believe in faith and religion when my father was torturing me." Father Daniel was silent. Things just got awkward. "And you aren't going to say a damn thing to me, are you? You're not going to provide positive spiritual insight—words that will help me reconcile these feelings?"

"Sure."

"Let's pretend this is a confessional and you're not in here to fuck me like one of your nuns, okay? Can we play pretend for a moment?"

"Okay." Father Daniel was a little worried about the doctor's sudden shift in tone, but perhaps this was part of therapy. A few moments of awkward silence ensued.

"So, you sit in the confessional and say nothing?" Astronelli asked.

"Oh, it was my turn to go?"

"Yes!"

"Okay, sorry. What am I responding to again?"

"My father torturing me!"

"Right. Okay. Here goes." He took a deep breath. "Everything happens for a reason, child. God has a plan for you. He will not allow you to suffer for long."

"That is total rubbish, Father Daniel. Could that be any more nonspecific? Do you say that to everyone in every circumstance? Better question: Would you say that to someone who had just murdered their father?"

"Oh, no."

"What would you say to someone who'd just murdered their father?"

"Well, I would ask why they did that."

"Because he was torturing me."

"Okay, I am so sorry to hear that. Would you like me to come with you to the police station to help explain?"

"Tell me if I'm going to hell for taking another human life."

"Not if you repent."

"How so? Ten Hail Marys? Twenty Our Fathers?"

"Oh, much more than that, I'm afraid."

"How much more?"

"I don't know. Okay, can we stop this little experiment now? I'm not really comfortable with this. I've never encountered a murder confession."

"Convince me there is a God, Father Daniel, like you convince your parishioners every Sunday at church."

Daniel was feeling very anxious, which was something these therapy sessions were supposed to ease. "Anyone who does not love does not know God, because God is love."

"Poppycock!"

"Poppycock? I haven't heard that word in years. Okay, how about this one: Lift up your eyes on high and see: who created these? He who brings out their host by number, calling them all by name, by the greatest of his might, and because he is strong in power, not one is missing."

"Nope, that's not convincing me. Tell me, your followers buy these readings? This is enough for them to believe?"

"Yes, they believe. But they already have faith. Otherwise, why would they be at church? I don't have to sell God; it's all abstract, anyway. And do I really need to believe to steer them in the right direction?

Probably not. But do I want to believe? Yes! I used to see it in their eyes—the faith, the belief—and I was jealous. And guilt-ridden. And then my eyesight was taken."

"And that wasn't proof of his existence?"

◎　　◎　　◎

The spray of bullets in the landfill forced them all to run for cover, and Father Daniel was left to his own defenses. He had no way of knowing where to run for safety, and nobody was helping him. He dove into a heap of garbage and assumed the fetal position, making his body target as small as possible. He wondered if the father-killing question was hypothetical, and as he lay listening to the gunfire and screams, he regretted not reporting the man above after his last session.

The *man above*.

Referring to the crazy doctor in this manner struck him in a profound way, for this man above was obviously not the God he sought.

And then a bullet hit a trashed item and created the sound of the church bell chime. It sounded as glorious as the evening chime that Daniel found so comforting— the chime that motivated him to pray and seek faith. And it struck him like the bullet that created the sound.

This was finally the sign.

In such a time of wickedness, the chime soothed him. Years of life in the church, including preaching and praying and helping people with their problems, flooded his mind, and he knew he had done well. He may not have carried on orthodoxly, but he absolutely had performed the work of God, and God was finally rewarding him.

The last bullet seemed to hit one of the dirt walls; it sounded much like a fist pounding into a punching bag. The crazy man above screamed something about needing more bullets, and Daniel heard the vehicle speed away. He crawled out of the trash and stood, analyzing the surrounding sounds. He heard Helen mourning over Beef, and Glen moaning, presumably, over what was still the pain in his arm, as Colin and Mia asked each other if they were okay. Everyone was accounted for.

Except Miranda.

"Miranda?" he yelled, bringing it to everyone's attention that she was missing. This was all he could do as he kept his sonar-ears on high alert.

Everyone quieted. They all seemed to flee in different directions at the start of the gunfire, but Daniel couldn't recall hearing about the blonde's journey.

"Miranda!" Helen screamed, to no response, as everyone began to scour the area surrounding their current locations.

Colin spotted a movement a few feet away and rushed to a super-sized trash bag and lifted it away to find Miranda lying on her stomach. He turned her over and saw her jeans soaked with blood. She was barely conscious as the group rushed to her side. Upon closer examination, Colin found a large gash on her inner thigh, but it wasn't from a gunshot. It was from the broomstick spear—the weapon she had created to kill the monster. It seemed she dove or fell on it, and it ripped into her femoral artery. She was bleeding to death.

"No!" Helen kneeled beside her and hugged her.

Watching Helen lose another of her favorites was going to be tough for Colin. He felt for the wound and applied pressure. She had no response to the pain he was sure she was in, indicating she was fading fast.

"Please don't leave me, Mommy. Please!"

Colin was a little taken aback by Helen referring to Miranda as her mother; the only explanation was the lack of nourishment and sleep. This many days in, they were all mentally incapacitated.

And then Miranda spoke in a slow, contrived manner. "I love you. You are a very special *little* girl. Please don't grow up before you have to. And know that you are loved by many. Never forget how special you are, you understand?"

Helen wiped a tear from her eye and placed her face on Miranda's bosom.

"Please, someone tell my kids I love them." Her voice faded as she fought to keep her eyes open. "Oh, and kill that fucking monster!" Miranda exhaled her final breath and closed her eyes as Colin pondered which monster she meant.

"No!" Helen sobbed. "No!"

Father Daniel began reciting last rites from the camp.

Colin gave the girl a moment to grieve, but that was all the time they had. The doctor would return shortly, probably with more ammunition. It was clear he wanted them all dead now. Colin wasn't sure why they hadn't all been killed before being flung into the landfill. Surely this man wasn't planning to rehabilitate and then release them.

"Okay, let's go, Helen."

"No!"

"Helen, I'm sorry, but we have to get out of the open. That man will be back."

Mia helped Colin pull Helen away. They covered Miranda's body in debris and headed back to base camp.

"We have to bury Beef too," said Helen.

Colin looked up to where the doctor was located only minutes ago, very anxious about what was going to happen when he returned. He wasn't sure they had time for the dog burial, but he decided to do it quickly to help the mood of the girl.

"Okay, fast."

Helen grabbed the butt end of Beef and Colin the head and neck. They walked him out a few feet, Colin kicked away some trash to form a partial ditch, and they laid him in it.

"Can you say your prayer for him? Please?" Helen asked Daniel, the nicest tone Colin had heard from her since the nightmare began.

Daniel recited last rites once again as they finished covering the German shepherd with trash and debris, and before the priest was finished with the prayer, Colin caught tears gliding down his cheeks from both of his deceased eyes.

◎ ◎ ◎

Ryan had awakened ten minutes after being knocked unconscious, mostly in the dark but with a ray of light shining through the broken closet door, hitting the wall behind his head. He was disoriented for a moment until the events of the morning replayed like a horror film. Blood dripped from his nose. And then he freaked, thinking the man in black was still in the house. He moved not one muscle; he barely breathed.

After several quiet moments, Ryan decided he was alone and stood. He grabbed the sleeve from a jacket hanging in the closet and dabbed his nose, soaking up the blood. And then he heard the gunfire. It was far but not too distant. He pushed the broken door to the side and stepped into the living room. He saw the shattered glass and the missing guns from the cabinet and made the connection. He peeked out the window and saw that the coast was clear—nobody scary outside. He pulled the front door open, stepped out, paused, and rushed back inside to search for a weapon. He prayed he wouldn't run into this man, or anyone else for that matter, but he needed to be prepared. He had no idea what was happening up on the hill of the old Carlyle Dump.

The popping in the distance continued. It could've been mistaken for fireworks if it were the Fourth of July or corn popping in a microwavable bag. He rummaged through the kitchen drawers, found a couple steak knives, and shoved them into his back pocket a little too hard, as they cut through the bottom of the pocket. He removed them and wrapped them in a moldy dish rag and shoved them in his front pocket.

The gunfire stopped.

As he fled from the cottage, he heard a vehicle approaching from the curved gravel road above. He knew he couldn't run down the road in plain view, so he cut across into the woods, thinking he would make the journey back to the main road that way. He berated himself for forgetting his cell phone. If Rebecca hadn't left, he would not be in these woods fleeing from a suspected murder scene and murderer.

After a quarter mile of thorny-brush and fallen-tree navigation, he stopped to take a breath. The wheels of an automobile that he wished he was in turned in his head. Jamal would believe none of this. By the time Ryan made it to civilization, there was a good chance the scene above would be clean. Besides, maybe it wasn't a murder scene. Maybe a deer had smashed into the cottage, bled everywhere, and ran back out, and the man was hunting it down, trying to shoot it to end its suffering. Ryan's ADHD mind raced, creating scenarios a reasonable mind wouldn't. The thing that kept nagging him was the threat of termination. He couldn't afford to not be working, being a newly single guy.

He needed proof to corroborate his story.

After a moment of severe heart palpitations, Ryan made the pained decision to head back to the cottage to investigate things further—to get the real story. He could hide in trees and gather visual evidence. The man didn't know he existed; it would be safe.

Two steps into his journey back, a large creature stepped out from behind a pine tree ten feet in front of him.

Ryan froze, unable to comprehend what he was seeing. The huge, dingy-white creature did not move. Ryan did not move. They were having a staring competition, and Ryan was close to losing. He was also close to upchucking whatever food was in his stomach.

The creature pointed at him and opened his mouth, emitting an ear-piercing scream that caused Ryan to scream as well. He turned and raced through the woods once again. Branches cracked and leaves rustled behind him. This beast was too huge to catch him. There was no way—

And then, just as quickly as everything else that had happened to him that day, he plunged into a large hole and slid into partial darkness. Light from above showed him that the hole was more of a tunnel, and he reached to the walls and pushed, continuing farther into the darkness with little effort, as this tunnel reminded him of a muddy water slide. He heard a thud behind him, and another scream from the creature. It was chasing him down this dark tunnel. Ryan slid into total darkness and then stopped moving; the mud had switched over to dry dirt and clay and ceased the slide. He got on his hands and knees and began crawling deeper.

The tunnel was not consistent in its circumference. At times, it was large enough that Ryan had about two feet above him and beside him, but other times just a few inches of extra space, forcing him to become a caterpillar. He crawled as quickly as possible, but it seemed this tunnel was never ending, and he was fatigued. And then he realized the creature wasn't screaming, and he didn't hear anything behind him, so he paused to catch his breath. The lack of air and physical exertion forced deep inhalation, pulling the aromas of the earth into his mouth, which weren't all that pleasant. After a moment, he continued, praying this tunnel led to some place safe.

Suddenly the tunnel felt larger: there was moving air, and his head wasn't hitting the top. He reached above him in the darkness and did not touch the earthen ceiling. He stood up completely and still didn't touch the ceiling. He stretched his dirt-covered hands and slowly spun to gauge the space. This action caused him to become lightheaded; being underground and unable to see was playing tricks on his body. He felt around the walls for another opening to continue his journey, fearing this might be the end of the tunnel with nowhere else to run.

He found a smaller hole and continued with his crawl. It gradually seemed to incline.

And then terror struck him as he realized his disorientation had sent him back up the tunnel he had just come down. He paused for a moment, overwhelmed by mental and physical exhaustion. He wanted to cry but didn't get the opportunity.

The beast was upon him, grabbing him by the throat and squeezing him to sleep.

THE PLAN

The not-so-good doctor knew of the Carlyle Dump from a woman he'd counseled a year earlier. Turned out the woman's abusive husband had tried pushing her into the hole after a fight while he was illegally unloading a truckload of empty paint pails and other toxic chemicals he couldn't throw in standard trash containers. Based on the therapy sessions with this woman, Astronelli believed she should've been tossed down there, and this gave him the notion to turn it into a human trash dump. Each imbecilic character who stepped into his office would have a special place in the trash hole. Of course, this was fantasy. It only turned into reality when he was off his medications and decided to kill his father. It was as if his father's evil spirit then took possession of his body and mind and compelled him to continue with the sadistic psychological experiments, only on a grander scale.

Hubert and Loretta were pawns all along. He didn't have a million dollars to give them. They were fools to ever think that. He figured he'd settle with them somehow or kill them. They weren't patients who needed healing.

Don't heal them. Kill them.

His escape would be easy: he would shave his scruffy beard, get a decent haircut, change his identity, and drive his car until he found a suitable small town he could blend into for a while, cash in hand to last him a year until the manhunt died down and people forgot about the incident in the old Carlyle Dump.

On day five, in the toxic hole-in-the-ground, the confessions would be heard. Patients would share their stories with the others, bringing guilt and shame, forcing them to evaluate their poor judgment and behavior. Afterward, they would be rewarded with water and a brownie, one of which was poisoned. Watching one of their group therapy members die would reiterate the need to change or face the consequences; it brought a sense of urgency. Following the first death, other sadistic games were planned—possibly resulting in another death—until each of the survivors was completely rehabilitated. Then he would flee, and if they ever escaped the hole, he'd be dust in the wind. A brilliant group therapy session to end all group therapy sessions, and the most rewarding aspect—it was better than anything his father had ever concocted.

And then a patient escaped. It now made more sense to cut his losses and move on. Since the therapy was cut short, and the patients weren't healed, he'd decided they shouldn't live. Altering the plan also meant he'd be safer when he moved; he'd have peace of mind and never have to look over his shoulder. Their bodies would never be found in the hole, especially after he covered them with dirt. Then he'd place a chain across the start of the gravel road with a *closed* sign to keep out any illegal dump bandits.

Kill them. Don't heal them.

The doctor rummaged for more bullets back at the cottage. He pulled out drawers and threw them; the contents flying everywhere, including dice, a deck of bikini-model-covered poker cards, screwdrivers, and packets of ketchup and sugar.

You've made a real mess of things, kid.

"I hear you, Father. We can't all be as flawless as you. I'm managing this situation. It might take a little time, but nobody ever comes around here, so I'm not concerned."

Why aren't you concerned about the escaped one?

"Because he's dead. Haven't you been following along?"

If one escaped, shouldn't you be concerned that others will escape?

Astronelli stopped throwing things and plopped down on the dirty, bloody sofa. He pondered the question his father asked. Before his death, was Byron ever in the hole? Had they established that? Or had he escaped from the van before he was even placed in the hole?

"They are all still down there. If there was a way to escape, wouldn't they all be gone by now?"

How do you know they're all still there? You're here. It's obvious that intelligence skips a generation.

"Will you please leave me alone? I have control of the situation."

Damage control was always your device. If you did things properly in the first place, you wouldn't have to clean up messes. You should've been a maid.

"I cleaned up the mess of your existence, didn't I?"

Astronelli snickered as he stood and continued the search for bullets. He got on all fours and looked under the sofa. He pulled out two old cigar boxes and opened them. One was stuffed with money. The other contained the skeleton of what appeared to be a cat. A piece of paper was taped on the inside lid: *RIP Trixie Lou.*

"Who the hell names a cat Trixie Lou? Total rednecks." He slid the cat carcass back under the sofa and grabbed the box with the money. This was his tip for dealing with Hubert's incompetence. A one-way ticket to Vodkaville would be purchased when he got off the mountain of death.

Are you killing them with kindness?

"Please leave me alone," he pleaded with the voice in his head disguised as his father. He rose and scanned the cottage for another source to introduce death to his patients. A box of rat poison sat on the counter next to a box of Little Debbie oatmeal crème pies. He grabbed a pie and inhaled it.

You sure you have time to get fat, kid?

Astronelli grabbed another pie and shoved it in his mouth, nearly choked, and then spit it on the sofa. He raised his middle finger in the air, as if his father were in the room, and walked to the bedroom. He continued his search for weapons or ammo, only to find underwear and stacks of Styrofoam takeout containers. He kicked the containers, one hitting the curtain and moving it a little to expose the outdoor tool shed.

There were murder weapons in the toolshed.

Stick a pitchfork in you. You're done.

◎   ◎   ◎

Rocka smelled more death and dinner. He caught the scent shortly after the bangs from above. The bangs that killed things. At this rate, he could stockpile food for a long time, eliminating the risk of searching for nourishment in the woods. He just needed an area to bury the bodies, keep them cool and as fresh as possible. But he didn't want to eat everyone.

He wanted a friend.

If he found a human who didn't run screaming or try to hurt him, he would consider making them his friend. He had no sense of time, but it had been a while since his sister died. Twenty-two years of human life. She was the last one in the family of five to die. Diseases were the number one cause of death for his species, as humans were too slow and dumb to be harmful.

"Hello?" the man said, his hands and feet tied better than the other man's—the man who got away only to die in the shelter above. Rocka had smelled his former captive's raw flesh when he was searching for him near the cottage. He was no longer scared the man would return with an army to remove him from his home in the earth.

"Who's there?" the man asked, lying on his side, his face resting on a small mound of dirt that Rocka used as a pillow.

Rocka poked him in the ribs. The man screamed. Rocka kicked him in the ass and moaned a little, his way of telling him to calm down.

"Look, I'm not going to hurt you. Don't be afraid of me."

Rocka moaned again, ending in a higher tone—a question mark of sorts.

"I'm cool with your kind. You have absolutely nothing to worry about."

This human man's tone was friendly and nonaggressive. And calm. The first time he'd ever encountered that.

"What is going on up above? What are you hiding from?"

The beast heard his new prisoner roll onto his back and bring his legs to his chest as he pushed himself up on his butt and leaned his back against the underground wall.

Rocka tried to communicate with him, making various sounds, some deeper pitched and some a little higher in tone. He was trying to explain why he lived in the hole, about his plight in the wild, and how he couldn't trust anyone. He wanted the man to know the only place that was safe now was his lair, that there was a crazy man outside he needed to hide from. He wanted the man to know he didn't want to harm him or anyone else, that he was mostly a gentle beast, unless his safety depended on violence. The man seemed to understand his sounds and signals, as he made a few similar ones in agreement.

◉　　◉　　◉

Ryan was more afraid of the dark than he was of the beast. It helped that he had always been fascinated with Bigfoot and yeti and the local legends, such as the Farmer City Monster—much like Bigfoot but with yellow, glowing eyes—and the Cole Hollow Road Monster; a three-toed beast with a thick coat of white fur that resembled dreadlocks. Others included the Murphysboro Mud Monster—a seven-foot-tall beast that lurked along the banks of the Big Muddy River—

and his favorite—the Rocket Mile Monster, spotted several times in the Rocket Mile State Park. Nicknamed Rocka, this beast was also covered in thick white fur and also had a cry that was almost alien. He read about a couple traveling through the park and almost running into the beast late one night. When the headlights shined on Rocka, he held up his hand and motioned for them to stop. The couple claimed he wanted to be sure they saw him, to not run him over, and he smiled and waved to them as he walked away.

Legends aside, his connection to these beasts ran personal. Growing up, he and his older brother bonded over them. They even created their own holiday to worship Bigfoot. Every October 25 they begged their parents to take them to the local park so they could explore the woods in search of clues to prove the large, hairy guy existed. They even made concrete molds of mysterious footprints, most of which turned out to be boot-print-deer-print mashups. Bigfoot Day would close with a viewing of *Harry and the Hendersons*. Once his four-year-older brother graduated high school, he found a purpose in life and moved away to do humanitarian and relief work in third world countries. Besides the Happy Bigfoot Day texts, Ryan hadn't heard from his brother in three years.

Ryan wondered if he was in the company of one of the beasts of local legends. The sightings were so long ago it hardly seemed plausible. And this one wasn't white. Maybe with time and living in the dirt, the fur had darkened. Perhaps he needed a bath.

"Rocka?"

The beast growled in the tone of a question.

"Are you Rocka? RooooKaaaa?" Ryan asked slowly.

The beast emitted what seemed like a laugh and swatted Ryan's ass. Ryan laughed in return in what could only be described as a surreal moment. He wondered if it was happening or if he was still in the dream with the trees and being lost in the woods. Huge hands grabbed Ryan's tied hands and started undoing the rope vines until a rustling from the tunnel above stopped him.

Something or someone was coming down the tunnel toward them, the sound indicating it wouldn't be long before it dropped into the main chamber. The beast swiftly left Ryan's side and made his way up the tunnel, never completely undoing Ryan's hands but loosening the vines enough that Ryan could finish the job. Once his hands were freed, Ryan stretched forward and untied his ankles.

A ruckus of screeching and squealing erupted, scaring the bejesus out of Ryan, motivating him to search for another way out. Although there was a weird connection with the creature, he certainly wasn't ready to become his roommate, even though he would be needing a roommate soon. He wasn't convinced Rocka could afford half of the rent. Ryan smirked as he envisioned the beast working the McDonald's drive-thru in his restaurant attire.

Small pebbles rolled down the tunnel and landed near him. Whatever was attacking the beast was doing so diligently, but surely it wouldn't win.

Ryan continued to feel around for another tunnel opening; the hollering from above ensured he'd go the right way this time. A moment later, he found another opening and started to crawl through it. He thought about his brother again, how he would've killed to experience this truly worthy event on Bigfoot Day. Twenty feet later, Ryan brushed his hand against something slimy and smelly. He guessed it was an animal carcass of some sort, and he was glad he couldn't see it.

Another ten feet and he could see the outline of his hands as well as shapes and shadows on the dirt walls. And then he fell five feet into a ditch—why didn't he see that coming? The aroma was rancid, but a few thin rays of light and hope of escaping the dark earth motivated him. He stood and pushed his hands above his head, lifting away a layer of something he couldn't yet identify. He saw clouds and was ecstatic, realizing he took the beauty of clouds for granted in normal times.

He squatted and pushed with his legs and feet, hopping out like a rabbit. He stared at the huge hole of trash before him in what was obviously the old Carlyle Dump. He had visited landfills before, so there was no question this was what he was standing in, but why wasn't it filled in? It'd been closed for nearly two decades. He scanned the contents of the hole and found typical throwaways, some illegal. But trash was all he saw.

And then he saw the crumpled body of an old lady.

THE CAMOUFLAGE

Survival called on them to return to where they had awakened two days ago: buried in the putrid waste of the dump in the ground. Would this prevent the crazy doctor from shooting them upon his return? Maybe not. If he realized they were hiding versus having escaped, he could just shoot everywhere and would probably hit one or two of them, depending on the amount of ammunition he found.

Each of them reflected on their lives and on how they had ended up where they were currently lying. Did they honestly deserve this punishment? Had they not learned or grown from the therapy sessions with the insane doctor?

◎   ◎   ◎

Mia recalled a conversation with the production assistant on the set of *Aces of Slade*. One of the producers of the show needed to speak with her immediately. She left the living room set and headed to Nigel's office on the third floor. He was an executive producer of five different shows currently in production across all platforms: cable, streaming, and broadcast networks. She'd never spoken to him one-on-one, and this made her anxious.

"Come in," he said in his English accent.

She entered the shiny, spotless office and closed the door behind her. He motioned for her to have a seat.

"How are you today?" Mia asked in her slightly seductive voice, a nervous habit when faced with an uncomfortable situation.

"Very well, thanks. Look, Mia. We conduct polls and follow social media chatter very closely here, and sometimes we're forced to make hard decisions based on this feedback." It was now confirmed: she had a reason to be anxious.

"I totally respect that, Nigel."

"People don't like you, I'm afraid. Season two has lost over a million viewers, and it seems to be your fault if I may be so candid."

"My fault?"

"People don't empathize with your character. You come across as unlikeable."

"Really?"

"Yes, afraid so. You are supposed to be the heart of this show. I mean, your character is supposed to be the heart, the moral center, and when that's missing, it all feels empty."

"I understand, I suppose. Why haven't I been directed differently then?"

"You have been, from what each director has told me. Look, Mia, we're willing to take some of the blame here. You were brought in a little young and inexperienced. But we have to make some changes if this show is going to survive."

"You can't fire me!"

"Yes, we can."

Mia stood and turned to the door. "You do know how I got this job, don't you, Nigel?" She turned back to him, slowly strutted to his glass desk, and sat on the edge. "I fucked your partner, Donald. Yep, that's right. You fire me, and I go to *People Magazine* and cry sexual misconduct and harassment. Hell, I'll even insinuate rape. With the current climate of sexual assault in Hollywood, I could have this production company shut down." She didn't share the fact that she enjoyed the sex and that it had happened more than once, she being a willing party to it all.

Nigel was stunned. He had confronted Donald frequently about sexual misconduct rumors, but they were always denied, and there was never any proof.

"You don't threaten me, young lady. Who do you think you are? Halle Berry?"

"Fuck no. I'm Halle Berry's worst nightmare. By the time my career is over, I'll have two more Oscars than that bitch."

"Wow." Nigel laughed. "Is it any wonder you come across as unlikable? Get the hell out of my office."

"We understand one another, right? Get me better directors if you want better performances."

Mia left the office, and Nigel threw his Emmy award across the room. It smashed a framed picture hanging on the wall—a picture of a smiling production staff, which included Donald.

They gave in to her blackmail under the condition she sought counseling for her misandrist ways. She did so back to her hometown of Shady Springs, away from the limelight of Tinseltown. Thus began her sessions with Astronelli.

And now she lay under rotten diapers and moldy clothing, hoping a bullet wouldn't enter her body and end the role of her life. If Nigel and Donald knew her current position, they'd surely be having the last laugh.

"The only reason I'm here is to keep my job," she told Astronelli at the start of their sessions. "I really can't expose those guys, or my career will be over. Thankfully, they bought my bluff, for now."

"Why the harm in starting a new acting job? Maybe something more suited to your skills. Maybe a black comedy?"

"Seriously? Do you know how much work was involved to land that role? I can't let it go. I may never act again."

"Sounds like you lack self-confidence, and you use sex to make up for it."

"No. Uh-uh. I'm not doing this with you. We will meet for five minutes each day, and you will sign off that I was here an hour. I'm not talking family and feelings and shit with you."

She now regretted taking this stance with him. Maybe he really would've helped her. And then she thought of her shooting schedule for the show. Not knowing how long she'd been gone; they could very well be waiting for her. She may very well be out of a job after all. On the plus side, though, someone should be out looking for her. Might they find clues to lead them to this shithole and her rescue?

◙　　◙　　◙

Thoughts of rescue filled Glen's mind too as he curled on his side, the bullet-injured arm facing up, a couple bags of trash on top of him. Each of the survivors was spread throughout the rectangular bottom of the pit, each hoping to claim a safe spot. Glen imagined them making the six o'clock news, particularly footage of his damaged body being lifted from the earth by a helicopter. He thought about the fresh batch of young interns and the e-mails from girls wanting to have sex with him, the poor wounded hero from the hellhole. And then he realized that line of thinking was the reason he was fighting for his life.

"I completely understand that I am selfish, Doc. I completely get that I am a person who is treated very well by my employers at the station and that I am loved by my wife and son way more than I should be."

"Your wife never confronted you about your infidelities?"

"No."

"What would you tell her if she did?"

"That she was crazy, of course. I certainly wouldn't admit to it."

"Wouldn't it make you feel better to be honest for once in your pathetic life, Glen?"

"Excuse me? Pathetic? You can't say that shit to me. You're supposed to be fixing me so I'm not pathetic, right?"

"How is that? You're still making the same mistakes you were making six months ago. We've made zero progress. You're not taking my suggestions to heart. You admit to having sexual relations with a new girl each time I see you. I don't get it. What do I have to do to get it through your thick fucking skull that you are destroying everything and everyone in your path like a tornado—that stupid fake tornado you point to during your weather segment on the unintellectual news? They may or may not know it yet, but it will come out, eventually. You're a fraud. You would be better off dead, Glen." Astronelli stood and turned his back to a shocked Glen.

"This is some sort of joke, right?" Glen chuckled nervously.

"No, it is no joke." Astronelli reached into a basket on the bookshelf in front of him and pulled out a gun. He pointed it at Glen.

"Holy shit!" Glen rose and backed away. "You are fucking crazy."

"Do I have to threaten you, Mr. Weatherman, to clean up your act? Should I tell you that the next time you step into my office you better have come clean with your wife and not had any more lovers? Can you promise me that? If you can't promise me that right now, I'm blowing your pathetic head off. Trust me. It'll be worth going to prison."

"Yes, I promise I'll do those things. Put the fucking gun down!"

Dr. Astronelli aimed the gun at Glen's forehead. "I don't believe you." He pulled the trigger as Glen screamed like a female pygmy goat. A flame popped out of the barrel. "Want a smoke?" The doctor laughed.

"I'm going to have your license, you quack!"

Glen grabbed his sports jacket and stormed out, slamming the door behind him. On his drive home, he realized it wouldn't be in his best interest to take any action. His wife did not know of the meetings, which were required by the owner of the television station after an intern reported his misconduct. She would start to ask all kinds of *why* questions if she knew. He was done with this man.

Or so he thought.

◎　　◎　　◎

Father Daniel reflected as well, as he was covered by a severely saturated oriental rug that was nearly suffocating him. He was closest to the edge where the doctor had last fired, but he was blissfully unaware of this, as the others had placed him there. He was still excited about the chime—the sign that God was up there and making his presence known to him after all these years. He was determined to survive and to project his newfound holiness. But would God allow him to survive?

◎　　◎　　◎

Colin was having a hard time understanding anything that was happening. His physical and mental weakness tried to consume him periodically. His insistence they would escape that day seemed ridiculous now. If they convinced their captor they had escaped with the implemented hiding plan, and if the madman fled, they might still have a chance. But when would he return? There was a good chance they'd remain buried for some time. His partner's fate and the scene at the emergency room felt like a distant dream, one he fought to remember. Had it even happened? He felt sadness at the thought of dying, of not fully realizing his true self, having just come out of hiding his sexuality five years ago. His family was still light years behind in understanding, and he wanted to work on that.

Colin had joined the coming-out-on-YouTube trend to inform his parents and younger sister. He shot the video on his Android phone and posted it to the video site. He texted the link to the video to his family on a Sunday afternoon, when he knew they were all lounging at home, so they could process it together.

And then he sat and waited.

And waited.

And then he was so worked up over not hearing from them immediately that he developed a case of the Hershey squirts. As he was sitting on the toilet, they called. In a frantic attempt to answer, the phone slipped from his hands and fell into the dirty water below. He shrieked, quickly fished it out, and rinsed it in the bathtub. After cleaning up the brown drips all over the bathroom floor, he blow-dried the phone, all the while nearly suffering an anxiety attack over not knowing what his family was going to say. It seemed his entire life had led to this response, and now it was tarnished in his shit.

The phone case prevented it from being destroyed. His family called back a short while later, and they all had a good cry on speakerphone. They assured him they loved him no matter who he chose to date. He already felt he needed to tell them he didn't *choose* to be gay— it chose him—but he decided to explain more in person, which he did. They certainly had some awkward moments while watching things together; the depiction of gay sex even made Colin a little uneasy. His folks tried to binge-watch *Will and Grace,* thinking this would help them understand their gay offspring, but they couldn't get through the first season. They hated Jack's flamboyance. And then Colin started dating a semi-flamboyant man named Jack. It took a year to introduce him to his parents. And another year for them to accept him and the dynamics of their son's relationship.

Colin thought about how weird and difficult it would be for family and friends of the couple to process the two of them dying in two totally unrelated acts of senseless violence.

Colin heard a muffled sneeze and for a moment thought it was Jack. He had a very high-pitched, shrilly sneeze. It wasn't Jack. It was Helen. She was having a sneezing fit, and Colin panicked, hoping it would end quickly—before the return of Dr. Death.

◎   ◎   ◎

Helen had something up her nose that instigated the sneezing fit. Something had crawled up her nostril—an ant, perhaps? The sneezing did end but not before she bashed her head into a concrete block during the final sneeze. She felt herself fading to sleep.

She awoke in her bed, the room lit by artificial stars. Her alarm clock also acted as a little projector, throwing multicolored stars onto the popcorn-plastered ceiling.

"Wake up, loser!" her buddy, Chance, said from the shadowy corner of the room.

She sat upright and peered toward the voice. Chance emerged, colored by the blues and reds of the stars. "Holy shit, you scared me! What are you doing here?"

"Der. I'm here to save you. You were having a fucked-up dream, right?"

"Yeah. I was in a—"

"Shit hole? Yeah, I know. It was a dream. You're awake and safe now."

Suddenly the opening beats of a Katy Perry song began, and Chance leapt onto the bed and started serenading Helen, jumping from her left to her right. She wasn't sure of the song: "Teenage Dream," maybe? And then he slipped and fell to the floor.

"Shh, you dumbass! My grandparents will hear you." Helen giggled. Sitting against the headboard, she couldn't see the floor. "Get up!"

"I'm trying," he said, but it wasn't his voice this time. When a figure rose, it was no longer Chance. It was Dr. Astronelli. "Well, hello there, little girl."

"What are you doing here? Where's Chance?"

"Chance had a *chance* encounter with a butcher knife. He won't be returning in one piece," he said, evil laughter following. "We have some unfinished business, little girl."

"Stop calling me little! I'm gonna be thirteen soon."

"You think so, huh? I have a feeling you're going to be dead soon. Never hitting that magical age. And really, do you deserve to advance another year? What good have you done in the last year? Murdering your grandparents' beloved pet? Flinging it on the roof of your neighbor's house like some sort of piece of trash? How about the lying and cheating at school?"

"I'll get better."

"When, little girl? When?"

"Starting now, I will. I swear."

"You do realize your grandparents have done everything possible to raise a caring, responsible girl, but you haven't been receptive. All you do is cry and pout about what you don't have instead of appreciating what you do have."

Someone knocked on her bedroom door.

"Dear, can I come in?" It was her grandmother.

"Please do," the doctor said.

She opened the door and entered, the hall light circling around her, giving her an angelic glow. "Are you okay, dear? Is there anything I can do for you?"

"Do you see the man standing next to you?"

"Would you like some hot cocoa? How about an ice cream sundae? Your grandfather is getting ready to make one right now. We have sprinkles this time, too."

"Don't you know where I've been? Kidnapped! This man kidnapped me!"

"Don't be silly, dear."

Dr. Astronelli reached out and grabbed Grandma's hair and pulled it up, removing her already severed head from her body. He swung his arm toward Helen, Grandma's dismembered head just inches from her face and still talking as her body fell to the ground.

"Don't forget we're going to see the doctor tomorrow. Since you won't talk to us about anything, you need to talk to somebody. It's the healthy thing for you to do."

Helen was horrified yet hypnotized. She couldn't scream or speak. Blood began to pour out of her grandmother's neck onto the bed and when she opened her mouth, her entire demeanor had changed.

"It's not our fucking fault your real parents don't want you. We don't blame them one bit. You're a pain in our asses, little girl. An ungrateful little snot."

The Katy Perry song returned, prompting Astronelli to jump onto the bed and lip-synch while swinging Grandma's blood-spewing head around by her long, gray hair.

Helen screamed and awoke, still buried and still miserable.

"Hello? Is somebody there?" a strange voice yelled from somewhere in the hole.

A new voice.

THE SCORCH

Ryan's head swirled. He heard what he thought was a sneeze, followed by a scream from somewhere in the filth; this wasn't a figment of his audible imagination.

"Hello?" he called out for a second time. "Look, I'm certain I heard someone down here." His voice echoed.

He couldn't believe what he'd been through in the last couple hours. From his plunge into the freezing creek, to his plunge into the landfill that was supposed to be filled in, plus, the crazy man in the cottage and the two near-death experiences in between. But the biggest revelation was the giant Bigfoot-like beast. Not a soul would imagine this story. Jamal would think he'd totally lost his mind.

The bloody bird tells no lies.

Ryan thought of the dead bird again and his mother's superstitious nature. She was so certain that everything happened for a reason and that there was a sign to be found for every question or situation that he was completely turned off to it. He'd laughed at her preaching these beliefs and refused to believe it until his cancer scare three years ago. He had been under the weather for about a month, feeling lethargic and withdrawn. His mother finally convinced him to go to the doctor, which resulted in sinus infection medications. After another month, he forced himself to be and feel well, hiding the fact that he still felt ill. And then one evening, while he was flipping through television stations, he passed a telethon for cancer. They were interviewing a young guy discussing his early symptoms of testicular cancer, and even though they were broad symptoms and could've easily been disregarded, Ryan took them to heart, gave himself a testicular exam after a hot shower, and discovered a pea-sized lump in his right testicle. Turns out he had cancer as well, but he made a complete recovery because it was caught early enough.

He no longer discounted signs.

A little girl popped out of the trash in front of Ryan, sneezing once again. He looked at her, and then at the dead old lady against the wall a few feet from her.

"Who are you?" the girl asked.

"Oh, my God. What the hell is happening?"

"How did you get down here?"

"How did *you* get down here?"

Another person stood up out of the trash. He looked vaguely familiar to Ryan. "Jesus Christ, will someone answer a fucking question?" he said and then screamed, holding his arm, seemingly in pain, as the rag covering it was soaked with blood. And then others surfaced.

"Why are you people down here? What is going on?" Ryan asked as the others undug themselves.

"Were you a patient of Dr. Astronelli?"

"Dr. Who?"

"No, not Dr. Who. Dr. Astronelli!"

"Oh, I see what you did there," Ryan said to the thirty-something guy as he smiled, instantly connecting with their sci-fi interests. An odd time for a joke, but mood-lightening seemed essential. Everyone quickly introduced themselves, another odd social formality in their current situation, but once Colin started, they all followed. "No. I don't know this doctor. Is that who was shooting a weapon? Was he shooting at all of you?"

They nodded. Ryan explained what had happened to him so far in the day: the man in the cottage who they identified as their therapist, and the tunnel in which he crawled through to arrive at the landfill. He pointed in the direction of the opening, again covered with trash.

"Oh my God. A way out!" They all started for the tunnel.

"Wait!" Ryan said. "Bigfoot or Rocka or some other monster is probably still in there. I'm not sure he'll be happy about us invading his home. I mean, there is a chance that whatever fell into the hole killed him, but it is mostly doubtful. Not sure a deer or raccoon could put up a fight. This thing is huge!"

They acknowledged that fact, and Colin shared their stories of the beast.

"We don't have a choice. That's our only way out of here. I say we take weapons and fight that thing. If we don't move now, we're sitting ducks. Ass-onelli will be back any minute. We're fucking wasting time!" said Glen.

"Let me go first. I seemed to connect with him. Maybe he will let us through," Ryan said.

They quickly gathered boards and branches. Mia grabbed the murderous broomstick. They started to follow Ryan to the hole and then froze in their tracks.

They heard the sick engine of a dilapidated vehicle approaching from above. It got louder by the second. They ran as quickly as they could to the covered hole.

Approximately ten feet from the hole, they all turned to witness a rugged, old truck diving into the landfill from the ledge above them. It all seemed to happen in slow motion. They saw the doctor in his previous attire—the long black coat, hat, and glasses—in the driver's seat.

And the back bed of the truck was on fire.

Ryan had learned enough in his training to know that fire and toxic landfills were a bad, bad combination. "Run! It's going to blow!"

He uncovered the hole and directed Helen to jump, but Glen pushed her out of the way and jumped in first. Helen and Mia then made it in before the truck smashed into the middle of the landfill and exploded, sending flames scurrying along the floor of the dump. Ryan turned to see Father Daniel, who had lagged a bit and then fallen when the truck exploded. He stood and ran two more steps.

The flames engulfed his body, taking him back down.

He screamed and then rapidly cried his last rites.

"O Lord Jesus Christ, most merciful, Lord of the Earth, I ask that you receive me into your arms, that I might pass in safety from this crisis." He got part of this out in between his shrieks of terror and pain, but after a moment, the pain ceased, and he heard the most wonderful sound on earth and then in heaven.

The chime.

Helplessly, Colin and Ryan witnessed the priest burn before they dove into the hole as the fire rushed them and consumed the trash. The others had made the five-foot jump up to the beginning of the tunnel. Even Glen propelled himself up with his one good arm, practically leaving them all in the dust, or smoke, as the burning waste created a thick cloud of toxic smoke that was making its way up the tunnel, trying to stop them from escaping.

The glow from the fire created a light source in the tunnel, but the quickly rising smoke prevented clear vision. Ryan yelled for them to keep moving, but Glen needed no direction; he was well ahead of the group, fueled by adrenaline. The pain he felt when he put pressure on his arm while crawling eventually became more of an annoyance. He wasn't crying out. He had a three-foot-long, sharp branch shoved down the back of his pants, and it almost speared his ass when he fell into the lair of Rocka.

A scream permeated the tunnel. It seemed the beast was unhappy.

"How far away do you think it is?" Mia asked Ryan as they all finally caught up to Glen in the lair. Before Ryan could guess, Rocka jumped down into his living room and stood in front of them. He emitted another cry. Mia screamed as well.

"Hi, Rocka," Ryan said coolly. "Look, everyone, stay calm. I think I can talk him into letting us—"

Glen rushed the beast with his weapon. Rocka snatched the branch before it could harm him and then grabbed Glen's injured arm and ripped it from his body. Glen squealed and fell to his knees, blood spraying everywhere. Rocka took the severed arm and began beating Glen with it. While this was happening, Ryan pushed the others through to the other opening of the tunnel, and they quickly crawled through the opening as Rocka beat Glen into a bloody pulp.

As life drained from Glen's body, he thought of the intern he had tried to hump before he was abducted. And then each woman he'd had sex with appeared before him; the flashes of their faces seemed to last forever. He never realized he had that many affairs. He'd stopped keeping track after fifteen.

The last face that appeared was his wife's. She looked so young and beautiful. For a moment, at least.

"You fucked four hundred and seventy-three women, Glen. Four hundred and seventy-three. Twelve of them were underage. I mean, sure, I knew you were having an affair here or there, but nearly five hundred? It's shameful, Glen. Absolutely shameful."

Rocka stopped beating and looked for a sign of life.

"I'm sorry, baby. I am."

"I'm going out on your detached limb right now to guess you've had so many lovers, because after they had you once, they never wanted your pencil dick again. I imagine you had a lot of unsatisfied customers, Glen. I certainly wasn't satisfied. Imagine my horror when you knocked me up and I realized I was stuck with that pencil. Why, oh why, couldn't it have been a Sharpie king-sized, chisel-tipped marker?"

"I know it's skinny, but I know how to use it."

"Bullshit, Glen. Bullshit. I hope you find some beautiful, young angels to carry on your infidelities in death. Okay, hairy beast, he's all yours," said Glen's wife to Rocka.

The beast continued the beating, but the man who'd tried to spear him was already dead.

Rocka knew he would be dead soon, too. His home was destroyed, and the smoke he consumed only furthered the toxic cancer already running through his body. He wanted to believe the sicknesses he endured throughout the years were because of a lack of nourishment, but he eventually realized that it was directly related to his filthy home. He coughed up blood regularly. Even a beast knows that is a bad thing.

Rocka nibbled on Glen's fleshy arm like a chicken leg, savoring the chewy skin and the salty blood until he passed out.

The Rocket Mile Monster was dead two minutes later.

THE CANNONBALL

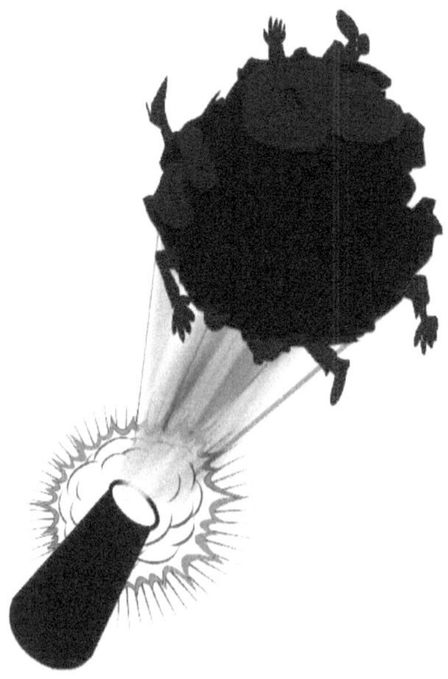

Helen was first in line. She was the conductor on the human train trying to find its way out of the earth station. Mia, Colin, and Ryan followed in that order. Together, they hoped to be the little engine that could. They all moved slowly, the smoke getting thicker by the moment and bringing a new, noxious level to the stench they had breathed for five days.

This tunnel of terror brought back one of Helen's earliest childhood memories: the play tunnel. When she was three, she'd been crawling around in the plastic tunnel—a birthday gift from her out-of-town aunt and uncle, now known as her parents. While inside the tunnel, she fell on her side, which caused the plastic tube to start rolling down a slope at the foot of the yard. Before a grandparent could catch her, she was on the street. A monster truck was flying by at the same time and swerved to miss the tunnel, but it still caught an end of wire and dragged the tunnel with Helen inside another ten yards before the driver realized what was happening.

Although Helen was too young to understand the severity of the incident, she'd never forget her grandparents' reactions. The fear and relief in their eyes resonated with her even to the current day—and knowing now that it was a gift from her real folks meant they had inadvertently almost killed their daughter. She was lucky to have survived.

She hoped she'd survive in this adult tunnel.

Coughing and winded, they were nearing safety as the daylight became brighter and the smoke began to clear. The mouth of the tunnel wasn't far away. This was their final hurdle, for it seemed the bad doctor had ended his life. He had driven the truck into the landfill and burned alive, much like the poor priest.

"Almost there," Helen announced.

And then a large explosion rocked the landfill behind them. It pushed gas and fumes through the tunnel with such force that the four remaining victims were shot out into the air like spitballs through a straw or a cannonball through a cannon. Their landings were the stuff of a trapeze artist's nightmares. Helen flew into a pine tree, her foot getting caught between the V-split of a branch and breaking her ankle. She screamed in pain as she hung upside down from that broken ankle, her head about ten feet from the ground. Mia landed six feet away in a thick patch of wood ferns, breaking her fall without breaking her bones.

Ryan head-butted Colin's ass, pushing him into the air and preventing himself from going airborne. He rolled a handful of times and smacked into a fallen tree as Colin disappeared from above.

"Help me!" Helen cried.

Ryan followed her voice as he regained his equilibrium. A bout of déjà vu squirmed in his brain, and he recalled the dream from what seemed like a mere handful of hours earlier. He found Helen dangling from a pine, buried a bit in the thick of the greenery. One look at her foot and he knew she was in terrible pain. The height of her wedged ankle was unreachable.

"Can you wiggle or move your foot any?" he asked and then realized that was a dumb question. He thought that she could release herself and that he could catch her. Dumb. He needed to get up in the tree, but there were no branches low enough to pull himself up.

"Oh my God!" Mia appeared, green wood fern guts all over her face. Getting a better look at her now, outside the hole, Ryan thought she resembled the woman in his dream—the one who knocked him from the tree and mounted him. She was certainly just as attractive—except for the plant mush and the landfill stench.

"Help me. Shit! This hurts!" Helen cried again, prompting Ryan to take a cue from his dream.

He jumped up into a neighboring tree and worked his way around to Helen's pine, leaping onto a branch above and working his way down to her branch. He tested the strength and decided to stay as close to the main trunk as possible.

"Okay, Mia, push the girl's body up, and I will twist—"

"No!" Helen shrieked, clearly afraid of the pain to come. The thought of her broken ankle twisting was unbearable, and she didn't even know it was shattered.

"I won't twist, okay? It will just release on its own. Okay, make your arms stiff so Mia can push you up."

With the girl's arms extended, Mia had a good foot to raise her, more than enough to release her broken ankle. Ryan's biggest concern was the branch. It was roughly three inches in diameter and a bit wobbly. He would also need to balance himself enough to lift her. He stood close to the tree, holding onto a branch above, the déjà vu returning.

In the dream, he fell.

"Come on, please!"

He took a deep breath and signaled for Mia to do her part. She did so beautifully. Ryan released the branch above and crouched, taking two small steps, grabbing Helen's good foot, and pulling her body up.

The branch buckled and began to crack.

Her broken ankle moved enough to release her, but the weight of the girl's body caused Ryan to lose his balance, forcing him to release her good foot, which sent her body crashing down onto Mia. The branch then cracked more and broke from the tree. He grabbed the branch above and hung in midair as the branch that had just held his weight fell fifteen feet to the ground below, barely missing the girls.

Crack.

"Move!" yelled Ryan, realizing he now had zero options but to fall to the ground.

Crack.

◉　　◉　　◉

Colin awakened on the gravel road, the tiniest of pebbles sticking into his skin in various locations. When he removed one from his ear, he heard Helen screaming from the trees. His immediate instinct was to jump up and run to her, but his body wouldn't allow it. He slowly and painfully stood and hobbled back into the thicket. On the short journey, he heard a few more screams and the snapping of tree branches. When he reached the clearing, all three of his fellow survivors were on the ground. Helen was crying and holding her ankle while Mia was straddling Ryan and apparently sucking off his face.

"I think he's dead," she said when Colin approached.

She evidently watched none of the countless medical dramas on television. You really don't want to jump on the victim's body unless you're on *Grey's Anatomy*. He pulled Mia off Ryan and kneeled beside him, checking for a pulse. He found one.

"How long has he been like this?"

"He just fell from the tree."

Colin began CPR. Ryan opened his eyes a minute later to feel someone's lips on his. When the head pulled away, he saw a very different version of his dream. He was getting it on with a man.

"Excuse me?" He sat up, recalling what had just happened moments earlier. He had the wind knocked out of him, literally. Colin just refilled his tank. "Oh, I get it."

"Can you stand?"

"Hello? Can you stop making out over there and help me?" Helen whimpered.

Colin gasped when she pulled her hands away from her ankle, which made her cry even harder. This was a reaction he was supposed to mute in the ER. Her foot was limp, lying on its side, while her knee and shin were facing up.

"Let's get her to the cabin. I think it's near here," Ryan suggested as he stood mostly pain-free.

He helped Colin lift her, and they carried her, each on one side of her with their arms wrapped around a leg while she held onto their shoulders.

"Are we sure that psycho is dead?" Mia asked.

"I saw him in the car," said Colin.

"So did I," Ryan said.

"But why did he kill himself?"

"Why not? It's no different from a mass shooting. The shooter blows away a dozen people and then kills himself. Same concept. Do you honestly think he thought he'd get away with this?" Colin explained.

Nobody really answered. They continued through the trees and made it to the road. Ryan steered them around the curve of the road until they spotted the cottage. A metallic-blue BMW Coupe was parked in front—the one that had appeared at the edge of the landfill frequently. Smoke from the landfill saturated the surrounding sky like a tribe of cumulus clouds. Ryan hoped the explosion and the smoke would alert a neighbor in the area, sparking a call to 911.

Mia pushed the door to the cottage open and gasped at the wrecked state of the inside: the destroyed furniture, the shattered glass and various colors of other broken ceramics scattered about, and the blood stains all over. "Oh my God. This man is a monster!"

Colin asked Mia to clear debris from the sofa, and they placed a calmer Helen on it. She was okay if she didn't look at the floppy foot. Colin took charge, directing Mia to find materials to make a splint and telling Ryan to search for a phone or car keys. His newfound freedom also nagged at Colin to find a way to contact a hopefully alive-and-well Jack.

After finding nothing in the way of keys or phones in the demolished living room, Ryan stepped into what was Loretta's bedroom and searched her drawers. Nothing but ancient clothing. He got on his knees and looked under her bed. It was stuffed with boxes and dolls. He pulled a porcelain doll out and inspected the little girl. She was dressed in a pink, gathered skirt, a cardigan sweater, and bobby socks. Cute outfit. And then he saw her face smeared with real makeup and lipstick. He wasn't sure if goth was a look in the fifties, but this child would've fit in.

He dug under the bed again and pulled out a photo album and leafed through it. A young, beautiful woman, who appeared to be an actress, was the subject of the black-and-white photos. Behind the scenes on a film set. Another photo of the woman in front of the Hollywood letters. Being new on the scene and not directly involved in the landfill proceedings, these findings didn't register with Ryan. He didn't know these pictures were of the younger version of the old, dead woman he first saw when he popped into the landfill.

"Anything?" Colin called from the other room, snapping Ryan back to the task at hand. He shoved the album under the bed and walked out, shaking his head. He continued his search in the second bedroom.

An old, now blood-stained, cuckoo clock cuckooed four times as Mia closed the front door, preventing the toxic smoke from entering. Outside had the look of a foggy morning.

With Helen's foot in place, Colin wrapped it with a roll of transparent tape, hoping it would hold until they found help.

"How far to the main road?" Colin said to Ryan.

"Not sure. Half mile, maybe?"

"Let's go. We need to get away from this smoke."

As they were scooping up the injured girl, they heard an automobile engine and crunching gravel. Help was arriving. Mia rushed to the door and swung it open.

A bulldozer appeared from out of the smoky haze, quickly approaching the cottage, bucket raised halfway off the ground, which prevented the operator from being seen. It was thirty feet away, and for a moment they believed this was part of a rescue party, until it got closer and clearly wasn't about to stop. Mia slammed the door, and Colin yelled for them to get to the back of the cottage. With Ryan's help, he grabbed Helen, and they raced to the kitchen and dropped to the floor, hiding behind the cabinets. Five seconds later, the bucket smashed through the front window. As Mia and Ryan screamed, Colin stood to get a better look.

Dr. Astronelli was alive and well.

"I'm so sorry, but your hour is far from up, which contradicts my normal way of thinking." The doctor chuckled as he entered the cabin and slammed the door behind him and it latched this time. The tractor was parked outside, and the large bucket still suspended five feet into the living room through the window and side of the cottage. "You know, I typically wish the session was over after five minutes of incessant self-absorption."

"How are you alive? Who was in the truck?" Colin asked.

"Just some loser who couldn't keep his hands clean. I believe his name was Byron. Yes, Byron. Quite a peculiar name for a man nowadays. Perhaps he was the last Byron on earth? Do you think that's possible?" Mia and Ryan were standing now, but Helen was still on the ground, curled in the corner under the kitchen cabinets. "Can you please, please tell me how in the good holy hell the four of you escaped?" The three looked at one another but didn't answer. Dust from above and pieces of the cracked roof of the cottage fell in front of Astronelli. "Time is short, and I really do not wish to repeat myself." He pulled a small pair of pruning shears from his back pocket.

Colin scanned the cottage and surmised the only way out was the front door, which was being blocked by Dr. Death. "A tunnel. A tunnel from the landfill to the woods," Colin said.

"Very good. Thank you. Assume therapy session on the sofa, Colin."

"I'm sorry?"

"Lay on the sofa, Colin. I'm offering you one final session."

Colin eyed the shears and rushed escape scenarios in his brain, looking around at possible weapons. The shears weren't that big.

The doctor, reading Colin's mind, pulled a gun out of his front pocket with his other hand and pointed it at Colin. "I didn't use all my bullets; do you think I'm nuts?"

"Yes," Ryan blurted accidentally.

Astronelli adjusted his gun hand and aimed at Ryan's head. "Who are you, and why are you here? You have never been my patient."

Colin stepped in front of Ryan; the gun now aimed at his head.

"I see. You're Colin's gay lover, aren't you? Did you come to save your homosexual sex partner?"

"I'll do therapy. Just don't shoot him, okay? It was an accident he's here." Colin trudged out of the kitchen and sat on the sofa, facing the doctor.

The gun was once again pointed at Ryan. "Does anyone know you're here? Give me your cell phone."

"I don't have it."

"I'm not asking again. Give me your cell phone."

"I left it at home. I swear to God."

Dr. Astronelli pulled the trigger. Blood sprayed against the pink tile backsplash as Ryan fell to the ground. Mia screamed and bent down to help him. "No, you don't. Up where I can see you, Mamma Mia."

Colin scanned the room again, looking for anything to fight this psycho with, but he was defenseless against a bullet.

"And don't look at me with those fuck-me eyes. You can't screw your way out of this."

"Oh, that's not the look I'm giving you, trust me." Astronelli aimed the gun at Mia's head. She screamed and fell to her knees.

"Get up. I'm not going to shoot you. You're my ticket out of here." He lowered the gun and looked at Colin. "What are you looking at? Lie down on your back and spread your legs, eyes to the ceiling, just like you used to do at my office when you taunted me with your stories about men."

"Taunted?"

You don't think I know what you did with that boy in your bedroom closet?

"I didn't do anything with him, I swear!" Astronelli's voice changed pitch. He was talking like a very nervous child. "We were talking about our new fourth grade teachers. Mr. Smith seems like he will be hard to learn from, and Mrs. Haley was just mean. It will definitely be an interesting year."

Put your hand around the bar, kid.

"Please, Dad. I didn't do anything." Astronelli started crying a little.

Colin, who was lying back on the sofa looking up at the ceiling, slowly turned his head to see what was happening without making it too obvious and provoking repercussions. The deranged doctor was in his own little world, his face contorted, fear and pain shining through.

You did something you will never do again. Put your Goddamn hand around the bar.

Astronelli raised the gun and, with his left hand, removed it from his right hand. He held it, pointing to the ceiling, and wrapped his right hand around the metal barrel, emulating the childhood trauma. Mia was watching, mesmerized by the surreal nature of his behavior, as Colin was about to seize an opportunity.

"Ouch, the tape hurts, Dad. What are you going to do?"

You're about to find out, kid. And trust me, this will hurt me more than it hurts you. But this is how we learn. This is how we become the men we were meant to be. Guidance and direction. We all make mistakes, Stuart. It is imperative to learn from it and never, never make that mistake again. Do you understand this? Stuart, look at me. Do you understand this?

His father flipped a switch, and the metal bar slowly began to heat. Stuart's hand was wrapped so tightly, and the bar was attached to a workbench, so there was no escape from the burnt skin.

Modern day Stuart Astronelli screamed as his right hand trembled, holding the gun.

Colin saw an opportunity.

He hopped off the sofa and tackled the doctor, knocking the gun across the room. They struggled on the floor, each getting in a few solid punches while rolling over the broken glass. Astronelli pinned Colin to the floor and started choking him, but Colin kicked him off and stumbled away. When the doctor rose to his feet, Mia was standing with the gun aimed at him.

"You found my dad's gun. Good!" He walked toward Mia, the childhood trauma and the flashback now behind him. "I'll just take that back now."

She pulled the trigger. No bang. No bullet.

"Oh, shucks. I only had one bullet left." He took a huge step and grabbed the gun from her hand and then pistol-whipped her. She flew backward onto the kitchen floor into Ryan's pool of blood. Colin punched him in the back.

"Kidney punch! No fair!" Astronelli tried to hit Colin with the gun, but he dodged it twice, falling back on the sofa. "Yeah, why don't you have a seat. Take a load off."

He pulled the pruning shears out of his back pocket. He dove toward Colin, who pulled his knees to his chest and caught the doctor's rib cage with his feet. He had a brief flashback to childhood and playing airplane with his dad, being lifted in the air by his dad's legs and seemingly flying. Instead of lifting the madman, he pushed him backward with the limited strength he mustered. It was a successful amount of strength.

Astronelli flew back into the bucket of the bulldozer and was impaled by the metal teeth. He dropped the shears and stared at Colin as blood filled his mouth and dripped onto the floor.

And there you have it, ladies and gentlemen: incompetence at its finest. Not only could Stuart not complete the task at hand, but he went and got himself killed. I've failed as a father in the land of the living, and now in the land of the dead, Stuart and I will have all of eternity to fix things. Together.

"Fuck," Astronelli muttered as his face fell forward, the last breath leaving his body.

Colin raced to the kitchen to survey the injured three. Ryan was alive and awake. Helen was applying pressure to his shoulder. The bullet had passed through it. Mia's cheek was lacerated, blood streaming from it. He bent down to help them.

And then they heard the sirens.

THE AFTERSHOCK

The four survivors completely recovered from their physical injuries, but the emotional scarring would stick around for a while. They didn't respond well when friends and family suggested they seek therapy, given their counseling track record.

Colin's boyfriend, Jack, had survived the nightclub shooting, and so had their friend, Jason. There were many injuries but thankfully zero casualties. The shooter was brought down by two drag queens. One knocked the pistol out of his hand with a high heel and continued to beat him with it while the other, a rather large specimen, repeatedly body slammed him.

Colin supported Jack through his lengthy recovery, their relationship transitioning to strictly friendship. Trauma did not equal a complete regaining of trust, and Colin realized he had a lot to learn about himself and his relationship inhibitions. They watched *Benny and Joon* a final time and Jack moved into his own apartment.

Mia left her hit cable show after meeting with the producers and apologizing for her sexual misconduct and outright blackmailing. She decided to leave Hollywood for a bit to focus on acting lessons and community theater. Being missing and victimized was like winning the lottery in her family. She finally received the attention she'd been missing all her life, and that was the missing ingredient in her dish of happiness. Six months later, she was asked to play herself in a TV dramatization of the landfill events. She won an Emmy award for her performance.

Helen's birth parents arrived in Shady Springs two days after she was admitted to the hospital. They were heartbroken and deeply regretted their decision to abandon their daughter all those years ago.

"Thanks for coming, Aunt Linda," Helen said after they ran out of conversation ten minutes into the first visit.

"Please. I'm not your aunt. Can you call me Mom?"

Helen was disturbed by this request, which struck her as odd since she'd fantasized about it for years. "No. I can't. I'm sorry. That's what I'm calling Grandma."

"But she's your grandmother. I'm your mother."

"For a day? Then you're gone again, right? What's the point?"

"We want you to come home with us when you're better."

"To Florida?"

"We want you with us, Helen. The thought of losing you was devastating." Helen looked up at the television on the wall, her head hurting. "Can you at least think about it?"

"Yes. I will."

"Thank you. We'll be back over tomorrow." Linda kissed her on the forehead and walked to the door.

"Okay," Helen said before she opened it.

"Really? You'll come?"

"No. I meant, okay, I thought about it, and there's no way in hell I'm coming to Florida. And if for some crazy reason you say you want to move here with me, I'll say no again. No, no, no. You are not my mother. You are my aunt, and I will continue to see you once a year or so. That's what I want. That's all I want."

"God. Your grandmother didn't teach you manners, did she?" Linda stormed out, slamming the door behind her.

Helen smiled, knowing she'd made the right decision.

The first thing Helen did when her ankle healed was ride bikes with her new boyfriend, Chance.

◎   ◎   ◎

Ryan not only got to keep his job, but he was also promoted to a position in the corporate office and deemed a hero, for if he hadn't arrived and emerged from the getaway tunnel, they all would've burned to death in that pit.

"Man, I thought you were nuts with all that talk about the dead bird being an omen. I told everyone the next day about that and laughed and made fun of you. Who looks like the fool now?" Jamal said as he sat next to Ryan's hospital bed the day after he was admitted for his gunshot wound. "I'll never doubt you again, my friend."

Ryan smiled. The dead bird omen could've referenced several things on that fateful day which led him to retire the omen theory. He realized if someone needed a sign, they could interpret anything as a sign. Seek and you shall find the answer.

Rebecca visited and told him how proud she was and that everything that happened proved he could take perfect care of himself. By the time he got home from the hospital, she had her stuff moved out of their apartment, and he was fine with that. They remained best friends.

A few months later, Ryan and Mia began dating; they saw each other weekly thanks to group therapy that all four survivors eventually agreed to attend.

◎   ◎   ◎

The cottage on the hill was leveled, and the gravel drive was buried. The Carlyle Dump was properly filled after the remains of the victims were excavated. Strangely enough, the remains of Rocka were never recovered. When the survivors told the story of the hairy beast, friends and family looked at them like they were nuts. It was a lack of nourishment or dehydration they were told, as their stories were dismissed. The only person who believed was Ryan's brother who finally returned home.

They continued to celebrate Bigfoot Day.

THE END

Thank you for taking the time to read this book. If you enjoyed it, please consider telling your friends or leaving a review on Amazon or the site where you bought it. Good word of mouth is an author's best friend and much appreciated. Bad word of mouth can go straight to the dentist.

ABOUT THE AUTHOR

Michael Evanichko knew he wanted to write from a young age. Reading the schlocky horror novels from the eighties ignited his warped imagination, which prompted his first attempt at penning a novel at age twelve. His passion for writing was the foundation for all his creative endeavors, culminating with the completion of his first full length, mainstream novel, *Life in a Supermarket Basket*. His follow-up novel, *Life in a Savage Landfill*, continues the story of a pivotal character from *Supermarket Basket*. The third novel in The Trilogy of Life, *Life in a Neon Knapsack*, was released in 2023, completing the trilogy. Michael currently lives in Tennessee, where he is hard at work on his next book, a gothic thriller.

www.MichaelEvanichko.com

MY SOCIAL MEDIA ACCOUNTS:

LIFE IN A NEON KNAPSACK

In 1986 with only days until summer break, high school freshman Mamie Blackhead finds herself under the path of a small exploding plane while walking to school. Fighting to avoid the raining debris she discovers a neon knapsack with a journal detailing the life of a boy who may have perished in the sky above. As she digs deeper into the journal she uncovers a mystery that will haunt her the rest of her life.